THE
GOLDEN BEES
OF
TULAMI

Other books by Frank Bonham

Chief
Cool Cat
A Dream of Ghosts
Durango Street
The Friends of the Loony Lake Monster
The Ghost Front
Hey, Big Spender!
Mystery in Little Tokyo
Mystery of the Fat Cat
The Mystery of the Red Tide
The Nitty Gritty
The Vagabundos
Viva Chicano

THE GOLDEN BEES OF TULAMI

FRANK BONHAM

E. P. DUTTON & CO., INC.   NEW YORK

Library of Congress Cataloging in Publication Data

Bonham, Frank   The golden bees of Tulami

SUMMARY: Determined not to give in to Turk Ransom's
pressure to join one of his gangs, Cool Hankins finds
unexpected support from an African stranger who seems
to be on a mysterious mission.

[1. City and town life—Fiction]   I. Title.
PZ7.B6415Go [Fic]   74-8295   ISBN 0-525-30765-6

Published simultaneously in Canada by Clarke,
Irwin & Company Limited, Toronto and Vancouver

Designed by Nancy Danahy
Printed in the U.S.A.   First Edition
10 9 8 7 6 5 4 3 2 1

CHAPTER

1

Late one afternoon in July, when the sky that had glared yellow all day was rusting into night, Cool Hankins was opening cartons of imitation orange juice in a rear aisle of Shapiro's Little Giant Market. Wearing a tan smock, he lifted the tall cans out of the cartons and stacked them neatly on the shelves, humming as he worked. It was a simple-minded yet somehow satisfying job. It brought in a little cash and gave him time to think of important things, like girls and money.

Cool was a high school senior and city boxing champion. School was serious business, but boxing was just a club he carried so that people would not mess with him. He had noticed that people only pushed you around if they thought they could take you. But if the word was out, *Don't mess with Hankins, he's a killer,* then everybody was your friend.

The truth, however, was that Hankins hated any kind of fight.

If an argument broke out at Sixth and Ajax, Cool was pretty sure to be cleaning his nails at Seventh and Elm a couple of minutes later. But these days, the story around Dogtown was that despite his good nature, he was a pretty bad cat; so most kids left him alone. His hook was as surprising as a sniper's bullet from an alley. His right cross was a bolt of lightning.

Finishing another carton, Cool straightened to ease the muscles of his back, jabbed twice at a juice can, and was making a right cross at a jug of cider when he saw three young men coming down the aisle.

Immediately he felt his heart sinking through him like a stone. The man in the lead was Turk Ransom, a very heavy dude in the gangs. The other two wore red jackets with the black Guardsmen emblem. Ransom was dressed in a pink coat, red pants, black cowboy hat, and lace-up boots, and his big sleepy eyes were focused on Cool. In shock, Cool wiped his palms on the seams of his pants, trying to remember how his alibi went. . . .

He was supposed to have called Turk last week. Turk had come into the store and said:

"Like to have you in one of my clubs, Monkey. What you say?"

What Cool wanted to say was, "Don't call me Monkey." They had not called him Monkey since he was ten, and climbing every pole, fire escape, and tree in the sprawling West Coast ghetto area called Dogtown, part of Coast City. But he said cheerfully:

"What club was that, Turk?"

"Name it, man—I got nine. Call me before Saturday."

Then he had wandered out, carrying two jugs of red wine without paying for them. Mr. Shapiro was cool enough not to remind him that he was supposed to. What grocer needed his store burned?

Cool had not called.

He had read a little in the Bible that night. He had

2

jogged a couple of miles every day, thinking hard as he jogged. But it was hopeless. There was no way out of it. He fell back on a childish prayer that Ransom, a very big fish, would forget about a sardine like him.

He did not want to join a gang and have the police leaning on him. Yet he did not need Turk Ransom leaning on him, either, for Turk was the leader of nearly three hundred boys in the Chain Gang family of fighting gangs.

Waiting for Saturday, Cool felt a fuse burning slowly toward a stick of dynamite in his life. Gangs had been as old-fashioned as flannel nightgowns a few years ago. But now, once again, they were running their roots out into all the grimy inner-city neighborhoods like poison ivy. All over Dogtown, boys were cutting and getting cut, shooting and getting shot, robbing, burning, dealing.

While across the dry riverbed where the railroad yards lay like a tangle of old plumbing in the wide wash, the Picket Fence family of gangs had grown even larger than Turk's. Picket Fence boys, and the girls who ran with them, sometimes drove over to the Chain Gang side of the river and cruised in broad daylight. That was against the rules.

It had been explained to Cool that Ransom was so busy with his drug business that he hated to take time for a gang war. But it sounded as though he was finally tooling up for battle by recruiting new members.

And now he was standing beside Cool again, smoking a bitter-smelling cigar that resembled a crooked black finger, and watching him shelve #10 cans of fake orange juice.

". . . Thought you was going to call me last week, Monkey," growled Turk sternly.

Cool said, with a nervous grin, "Yeah, well, see I—I got hung up, man, I—"

The other two men stood close behind him, one chewing on a toothpick, the other scratching his chin with a thumb. Their faces were as blank as play-dough. Turk turned away from Cool and squatted to lift two half-gallons of wine from a bottom shelf. Then he rose and confronted Cool once more. His face was long and somber, like a mask of polished bone. He made the twisted cigar fume.

"So what you saying to me, Monkey?"

"Hey, can we talk about it?" Cool said. "See, I was in a gang once, and—"

"Call me after you get off work tonight. Dig?"

He walked off without waiting for an answer. Why wait? The only music he ever heard was a diminishing hallelujah of yesses.

"Sure, man," Cool muttered. Turk turned back, his face blank. He frowned as if puzzled by Cool's statement, then shrugged and sauntered on to the cash register.

"How're you, man?" he said to Mr. Shapiro.

They conversed for a moment, their voices dropping so that Cool could not hear. Finally the gang men went out.

Well, that's it, Cool figured. He sighed and trudged to the storeroom.

When Mr. Shapiro counted out his pay that night, Cool fingered the bills slowly. "That's three dollars too much, isn't it, Mr. Shapiro?" he said.

The pupils of the grocer's eyes, tiny and pale behind thick lenses, darted about like guppies. He seemed very uneasy.

"Never mind, my boy," he said. "I'm afraid it's cut-off money. I've got to let you go. You see, one of my nephews—well, you know him, little Nathan—"

Cool frowned. Nathan was in the market a half-dozen times a day for candy and cokes. But he was only twelve. Mr. Shapiro continued stammering something about keeping the money in the family by hiring Nathan.

"Here! Take these loaves of bread to your aunt, Cool!" he exclaimed suddenly. "They're day-old, but she can use them at the foster home—"

"Okay, Mr. Shapiro. Thanks."

Sad-eyed, Cool carried the twenty loaves of bread to his car in the vacant lot beside the little brick building. It was eight-thirty. The warm air lay heavy as fog, perfumed with spices from a barbecue in someone's back yard. As he stowed the bread in the back seat of his old Buick, he sighed, with an intuition of further trouble. Turk had got him fired to make the point clear that the hook had been set in him like a trout, and until he got landed, Cool's life would grow increasingly difficult.

He heard the telephone ring inside the store. As he closed the car door, Mr. Shapiro ran out in his apron and waved like someone flagging down a taxicab.

"Telephone, Cool!"

Cool went back inside. Probably Aunt Josie, wanting him to bring something home. She had a big old, three-story wreck of a house where she was licensed to care for eleven foster children, and was currently carrying fourteen, not counting Cool. So it was always, "Bring another two gallons of milk, Cool," and "You didn't forget the corn flakes, did you?"

The telephone rested on the counter near the cash register, the handset lying beside it. Cool picked it up. "Hello."

"Thought you was going to call me when you got off, Monkey," said a familiar voice.

"Man, I just *got* off! I was going to call from home."

"I meant for you to call from the store, man. Man, I've got all the patience in the world, but this is ridiculous."

Cool clenched his fist, wishing, since wishing was free, that he had Turk in the ring. He closed his fist hard enough to crush a coke bottle, but kept his voice deadpan.

"See, the way it is, Turk, I have to help my aunt with the bills on her foster home. She's boarding fourteen kids, and only getting paid for eleven. She collects stray kids like some people collect alley cats. So I felt pretty bad when I got laid off tonight."

"Man, I was trying to *help* you. The bread ain't in peanut-size grocery stores. If you wanted money, you could drive down to Tee-wonna and make two hundred a trip. Put the dear old lady in fifty-dollar minis and a blonde wig."

"Or do five years if I got caught with Mexican cocaine in my gas tank."

"Say what?" Turk's voice went soprano in indignation. "Hankins, I don't deal no co-caine. And I'm getting tired of people asking me about co-caine. I don't know who's dealing on my turf, but it's gonna stop."

Cool did not comment.

Turk continued smoothly. "Now, Hankins, I'm going to tell you something about yourself. You are going into pro boxing, and you are going to make out like a bandit."

Cool groaned, his face screwed up in pain. "Oh, man, listen! If that's all you want me for—! I lucked out on All-City, but there isn't a pro in town couldn't knock my head off."

6

"Monkey, you are the world's Number One worrier. I'm going to bring you along *cool*—professional trainer, silk trunks—the works, baby! You want a girl? Point her out. Man, you travelin' under my colors. Hey, listen, a couple of dudes will be waiting to explain it to you over at Walnut Street playground at nine o'clock tonight. One of them is my main man, Mr. Clean, president of the Businessmen. You be there now, Monkey."

With a sigh, Cool let his weight down on the counter on his elbows. He heard the bell ring for Round One. An old animal with a face like chopped meat, on the way down but still dangerous, came shuffling eagerly from his corner to sniff around for him like a blind bear.

It would be worse than a traffic accident.

"But see, Turk—"

The telephone snarled like an angry bee in his ear.

Turk had hung up.

CHAPTER

2

Gloomily, Cool headed home for supper. The area known as Dogtown was made up of a dozen small communities—black, brown, Asiatic, white, mixed. Blocks of small homes sprawled between a range of lumpy hills and a wide concrete riverbed called The Wash, where trains flowed instead of water. Freeways cruised the vast area in arcs a child might have made with a rubber ruler.

In the early night, he turned up Ajax Street, passing clusters of bars, small businesses, and a police station. All the buildings except the police station looked bleak and temporary, like ramshackle movie sets. He turned up Hilltop Drive toward home, passing big old houses, the ghosts of mansions, clinging to steep hillsides overgrown with palms, pepper trees, and jacarandas standing in pools of purple blossoms. Between the houses were old cars, refrigerators, and anything else the trash man would not haul away. But tangles of geranium and cannas overflowed into the alleys, so that a migrating bird might conclude, from all the blossoms, that he had reached Central America.

He parked before a three-story house that resembled a stranded steamboat, all scrollwork and spindles. A warm breeze rattled dead fronds in the palm tree before the house. In the dark, a yellow Chevrolet body on the lawn, a swarming kid-hive all day, stood as empty as a dead beetle-shell. Lights glowed in the dining room. An aroma of spaghetti lifted his spirits a notch as he went up the walk with five loaves of bread under each arm. Ten loaves remained in the car. As he drew the screen door open and stepped inside, something flashed between his ankles. He grunted, tripped, and fell flat on his face. The loaves of bread rolled about like basketballs.

A boy of about seven whooped with pleasure. He dropped the broomstick with which he had tripped Cool. "Man, you so dumb!" he yelled, scrambling for the safety of the stairs. He wore a bath towel as a cape, and a space helmet with one antenna broken off.

Cool roared after him: "Marvin! You rotten little—!" Sitting up, he rubbed his shin. "You're going back to Boys and Girls Aid—I really mean it this time!"

Marvin vanished into the shadows of the second floor.

Muttering, Cool collected the loaves of bread. He limped through the dining room, where his aunt was serving dinner. She was a small, handsome woman who was plugged into some unbelievable mainline of energy. "What was all the noise, Walter?" she asked.

"That Marvin—he's got to go!" Cool growled. "He tripped me with a broomstick. Look at my shin." He pulled up a pants leg.

Aunt Josie clucked in sympathy. "That scamp. But it's *so* important right now that he knows we *want* him. He's been pushed around from pillar to post."

"Want him! Like scarlet fever, man," Cool retorted.

His aunt smiled. "Guess what he drew in his tablet today? Superman! And under it he wrote: *My Uncle Cool*. Of course it wasn't spelled right, but he really loves you. He just can't tell you, that's all."

Cool glanced down at his shin. "One of the great all-time lovers, I'll bet." He dumped the bread in the kitchen and went to wash up.

At dinner, Marvin sat between Aunt Josie and Cool, where he could not get at any of the other children. The oldest, Diana, was fourteen, and the youngest was four. Marvin refused to remove his space helmet, so that he had to raise a plastic gate each time he took a bite. A couple of the children were in high chairs. On the table, plates of bread and butter and cartons of milk were being shuffled about like counters in some very fast and sophisticated game.

Aunt Josie kept order, eating fast and talking to Cool. ". . . But if I ask for A.F.D.C. money on the new children," she said, "they're going to say, 'But you're only licensed for eleven kids. You'll have to put in another bathroom and—' Sue, will you help John?"

Marvin cocked his thumb and shot three children dead.

Cool belted down some coffee.

"What do you think about me going into pro boxing?" he asked his aunt. "Somebody wants to sponsor me."

Aunt Josie rolled her eyes toward heaven. "I promised my dead sister, your poor mama, that if ever you started acting like a loony, I'd have you committed. That day has come, Walter. Boxing!"

"Ever hear of Turk Ransom?"

"I don't go to the kind of places where they talk about the likes of him."

In other words, she knew who he was. Cool told her some more about Turk and of the hoodlum's interest in sponsoring him.

". . . So I guess he must want me pretty bad."

Aunt Josie's eyes showed pain, the way they did when one of her kids fell down the porch steps. She lived in Dogtown and knew how things were—which lines you stepped over, which were Federal offenses.

"We're going to have to put on a mother's march and run that trash right into the Pacific Ocean," she said.

"Turk isn't above drowning a couple of mothers," said Cool, "if they tried to spoil his circus. I'm going to talk to Breathing Man tomorrow."

"Do that, Walter. First thing."

A few minutes later, Cool left for his rendezvous with Turk's main man.

CHAPTER

3

Along Walnut Street, palm trees stood like discouraged panhandlers. Cars sped along a freeway across from the playground. Cool parked and looked at the playground lights sparkling through a glitter of dust. The main building was in the old California mission style, low and lumpy, like something kids had built out of mud. The baseball diamond was in darkness, but near the building strings of lights illuminated tattered volleyball nets and pipe-frame climbers. From the building, terraces climbed a hillside, with ping-pong tables under bare lights.

Two Chicano boys were playing at one of the tables. At another, a couple of young blacks were swatting the ball back and forth with a hollow clacking. A third man lay full-length on the cement retaining wall. He spoke, and both players glanced down as Cool took a seat on a bench near the building.

He could see them studying him. One player was tall and skinny and wore yellow pants and high platform shoes. The other man had to be Mr. Clean, for he looked just like the giant in the old television commercial. His head was shaven, and he wore a black muscle-shirt and black-and-white striped pants. Obviously he was a weightlifter, because his shoulders were grotesquely broad and his biceps were so enormous they would have ripped the sleeves out of an ordinary tee shirt. He looked like a Moor of the old days who would chop off heads for a living.

Mr. Clean tossed the ball in the air and smashed it like an eggshell, then tossed his paddle onto the table. "Company coming, Sprinter. Bread, you want to wait in the car?"

The giant and the thin man came down the steps, stopping near Cool to light cigarettes. Cool rose, smiling uneasily, and offered his hand.

"Hi. I'm Hankins."

The leader of the Businessmen transferred his cigarette to his left hand, then crushed Cool's hand in his right like a handful of potato chips. Cool kept grinning.

"Sure, sure, know you well, Hankins," said Mr. Clean. "Seen you fight, man. This is Sprinter McGaw."

They shook hands, and Sprinter offered Cool a cigarette. But Mr. Clean indignantly slapped the package to the ground.

"You off your gourd, man? This dude's in training. He totally clean, ain't that right, Hankins?"

Sprinter picked up the cigarettes as Cool gave a sickly grin. "That's right. You a pretty healthy-looking animal yourself."

Mr. Clean fondled his own biceps. "I lifts the weights some. Got started when I done time in Juvenile Authority. Them joints are zoos, Hankins. I decided I better be the strongest animal in the zoo. Of course I always been naturally big-boned," he added modestly.

They sat on the bench in silence. Cool cleared his

13

throat. "I was hoping you could square things for me with Turk," he said.

The shaven giant regarded him in surprise. "Oh, you got troubles with Turk?"

"Not exactly. He was wanting me to join one of his clubs. But I can't really see myself doing it."

"That's too bad. What club was you thinking of joining?"

"Well, see, what I mean, I wasn't."

Mr. Clean shook his head. "Can't understand you having troubles with Turk. He's the baddest cat I know. We does such a volume of business with him that everybody in my club got a real nice set of wheels."

"I dig that. But me, I was in a club, once, and I finally did six months in honor camp. And the way it is now, I've got to help my aunt with her foster home. Turk was talking about me fighting under his colors, but I'm not really that great. It might make the whole Chain Gang family look bad if I, you know—"

Mr. Clean watched him in puzzlement, as though he were a pitiful schoolboy stammering out an oral report. "Don't know why you *resisting* it so," he said. "Turk had a professional trainer watch you fight when you won All-City, and this man said you got a great future." His hand came down on Cool's thigh in a stinging slap.

"Great future in dentistry," sighed Cool, "if I get all my teeth knocked out."

Sprinter leaned forward to scrutinize him. He spoke presently, with smoke leaking out of his mouth as though his lungs were on fire. "You say you a pretty classy heavyweight, huh?"

"Light-heavy. No, man, *I* didn't say that. I'm just average."

"'At's what I been telling Turk. In fact, I like to see

14

you mix it with Mr. Clean, right now—bare-fisted! He ain't that bad himself."

Mr. Clean bounced up and sparred around. "Hey, baby, on your feet! Let's see if I can deck you. Only you better not tag me, dude—"

They were sparring before Cool could talk his way out of it.

Cool kept backing off. He knew he could take the muscle-freak in a fair fight, though he was outweighed forty pounds. For with his ridiculous physique, the gang man was wrapped up in a blanket of slow and ponderous muscle, and it was obvious as he shuffled around, his cigarette bobbing in his lips, that he was pathetically slow. He would set himself, then lash out viciously at Cool's jaw. Cool would tilt his head and make him miss by six inches.

As they sparred, the gang man began to scowl. He spat out his cigarette and started maneuvering Cool against the wall. But Cool darted around like a trout. He skipped on the packed earth, toe-tapping, stopping to drop his guard and take a step backward; then sidling in to rake a light slap across Mr. Clean's jaw. He shuffled and bobbed and slapped, until after a full minute of it the gang leader was sweat-drenched and gasping.

Mr. Clean suddenly dropped his arms, sucked in a breath, and grinned.

"Yeah, you ain't bad, man. So I tell Turk you with us, huh?"

"No, man! Tell him I'll think about it tonight, huh? I'll call him in the morning."

Mr. Clean took the lighted cigarette Sprinter handed him. "You don't need to do that, baby. Turk gave me a message for you. He said, 'Tell him he's either with me, or he's against me.' "

15

"But that ain't so! I'm *not* against him—"

"*Turk* thinks you is. *I* think you is. So I guess you is."

Cool called after him, "Hey, where can I call him tomorrow?"

"Call him at Brother Marvin's Card Room. If he ain't there, they'll take a message."

Cool saw the broad back disappearing into the shadows of the pepper trees. He stuffed his hands in his pockets. "Yeah, man. Thanks a lot."

Cool sat in the shadows until he heard a car depart with deep burbling noises like a speedboat. No doubt about it: There was no hope left except maybe in the wit and wisdom of Breathing Man. He was tempted to talk to him tonight, but knew he'd be asleep at his little camp in the storm drain.

He walked back to his Buick and climbed under the wheel. He pumped the gas pedal, turned the key, and heard a *pop* under the hood, like the report of a small firecracker. A little smoke leaked out. With a great pulse of fear, he hurled the door open and fell into the street, ripping his hand on a piece of broken molding. He scuttled away like a crab. As small a sound as it had been, it told him that it was probably already too late to escape with a whole hide:

A bomb of some kind was bunching its muscles under the car.

CHAPTER

Cool sat on the curb watching a fireman in a short rain-coat squirt water inside the smoking carcass of the Buick. The man was trying to extinguish the upholstery so that the engine crew could get back to their television program. Another fireman was prodding at the cushions with a bar. The engineer, standing beside the fire truck, said:

"Funny—it smells like toast, don't it?"

"It is toast," Cool said. "Ten loaves of toast."

People standing around watching the action made jokes and laughed. "If you had a pound of coffee in there," a man said, "we could dump it in the radiator and have us a snack. Was it your car?"

"Uh-huh. Anybody want to bid on a 1962 Buick fixer-upper?"

The bomb, praise the Lord, had been merely a fire-bomb, not dynamite. Otherwise, Cool might be lying on a table at General Hospital while a puzzled doctor said:

"I think this part with the wrist watch on it goes over there, Tom," and his assistant said:

"No, no, Fred—it's a *left* hand—it goes on your side."

Mr. Clean was right: Turk was a very fair man. He could just as easily have had Cool blown to shreds, but instead he had been content to issue another warning. Or perhaps it only proved how badly he wanted Cool.

Tomorrow he would say to Breathing Man:

"Breathing Man, I've decided to join the Businessmen and fight professionally. What do you think?" And perhaps the old man would come up with a good suggestion, like, "Don't do that, Cool—move to Yakima, Washington."

An unmarked car arrived with tall aerials whipping. The driver parked it behind the fire truck and got out. He was enormously fat, and Cool decided he could hardly be a plainclothesman. Carrying a camera, he waddled up and looked at Cool's car. Then he looked at Cool, sitting on the curb. Finally he called to one of the firemen:

"Hey, Cassidy, what gives?"

"Ask the boy, Tiff," said the fireman.

The man called Tiff came over and sat on the curb beside Cool. "How'd it start, sport?" he asked. "Cigarette?"

"I don't know. What's the difference?"

The fat man took a picture of the Buick's smoking ruins. "The difference is that I'm a newspaper photog and I've got a few minutes to kill between murders. I picked up the call and thought I'd cruise over. My name is John Tiffany. What's yours?"

"Walter Hankins. Um, listen. There's no big story in it. It's just—you know—old car—bare wires or something."

Tiffany scrutinized him. "Sure. Hey, haven't I seen you before?"

"I don't know. I don't live near here."

"Neither do I. Got it! I took a picture of you after a boxing match. Walter Hankins. All-City title."

"You've got a good memory."

"That's what makes me so valuable to the paper." Tiffany lowered his voice. "Better let me give you a ride home. If they take your name, you'll be charged for hauling the carcass away."

"I know. That's why I didn't want you to do a story on it."

Cool walked with the fat man to the newspaper cruiser. Tiffany opened the trunk. Inside, in a welter of photographic equipment, were a portable red ice chest and a couple of cartons of candy bars. Tiffany opened two cokes and handed one to Cool. He also gave him a candy bar and shoved one in his coat pocket.

"Get in, Champ," he said.

They started off. "Well. So," he said. "You don't know what started the fire."

"I tried to start the car, and I guess the carburetor flooded."

"No doubt. The reason I asked, I saw some gang punks getting the hell out of the area just before the fire call came in over the radio. I thought—you know, I drive around all night, I get so bored I make up stories."

Tiffany's fat face glistened as he smiled at Cool. He took a big bite of candy.

"I don't know anything about the gangs," Cool said. "Turn left at the next cross street."

The newspaperman parked and Cool got out. Tiff pulled out a billfold.

"Here's my card. So listen, if you ever need anything, Champ—I'm interested in everything that goes on, you might say, and there's a one-way zipper on my mouth when anyone tells me anything. Dig?"

"I dig. Thanks a lot."

"I'm sorry about your car. And I mean it about calling if I can ever help you. You know?"

Cool nodded. He knew all right. Knew he was being hustled. Also knew he'd never see John Tiffany again.

In the morning, Cool awoke swollen-eyed in his stuffy attic room. The hivelike hum of fourteen children at breakfast two floors below came faintly through the walls. No central idea lit his mind, but he had an ominous feeling, like cobwebs on the face. Turk. Mr. Clean. The flat clank of a bell, the smell of oil of wintergreen and sweat, and Round Four coming up. His manager whispering:

"We've got him, Champ! His knuckles are bleeding."

Cool opened his eyes and gazed gloomily at the rain-streaked wallpaper of the ceiling. Pictures of girls were tacked to it, all of them plump and healthy, and looking as though they were about to say, "Honey, why didn't you call?" He sighed and gazed out the window. Against a soiled sky a jacaranda tree was sketched in sharp, sticklike strokes and tufts of purple flowers.

He dressed and went downstairs. At the breakfast table, Marvin, wearing his space helmet, had just emptied a pint bottle of syrup over his pancakes, leaving none for anyone else. "Anybody kin be slow!" he yelled.

"Marvin, you little scamp," Aunt Josie sighed.

Cool banged his hand down hard on Marvin's helmet. Marvin tried to hit him. "I'm going over to the Pastime," he told his aunt.

"What are you going to tell that trash?"

"Won't know till I talk to Breathing Man."

He jogged through the hot morning toward the Pastime Pool Parlor, where Breathing Man spent his days. Cool had decided he might as well resume training, just in case. He arrived at the pool hall on Ajax Street scarcely breathing hard. The old boy called Breathing Man, whose real name no one knew, was propped against the brick wall in a straight-backed chair, one hand wrapped about a frosty beer can and looking like a blackbird's foot.

Winter and summer, because of a morbid fear of colds, he wore a surplus Army overcoat, a knitted G.I. cap, and a muffler. Years ago he had suffered an illness that had chained him to his bed for a year, and freed him finally, thin and frightened, and with the curious notion that unless he concentrated on his breathing, his lungs would collapse like paper bags—Poof! Pop!—with a dying whistle.

He had heart, though. He hurt when you hurt. He was happy when you told him about your new girl or new job. Summers, he lived in one of the city's huge underground storm drains, where he had a little camp and fed twelve or fifteen sewer cats. He had helped Cool with a lot of problems in the past, but as Cool gazed at the dark, faintly smiling mask of his features, he knew it would be a miracle if he could help him this time.

"Hey, there, Breathing Man!" Cool said.

The old man's eyelids raised. He smiled. "Well. How are you? Old buddy?"

Cool squatted on the walk. With a handkerchief, he wiped his sweaty face. "Got bad trouble."

Sipping a little beer, Breathing Man sighed. "I know. Heard about it. It's rotten."

Cool laid the whole story on him.

"So how do you say no to a dude like Ransom? He can raise a finger and have my head shot off. What am I going to say to him this morning?"

"Think of it. Like a fight. Is he bleeding anywhere? Hit him there. Open it up."

"*I'm* bleeding; *he* ain't bleeding."

Breathing Man's head turned this way and that, searching the walk. "According to what I hear. He's gonna be bleeding. Before long."

"How's that?"

Anxiously studying the lined and leathery mask of the old man's face as he tilted the can to let an icy brook of beer go trickling down the hot summer of his throat, Cool felt a flutter of hope. He was placing a lot of faith in those wrinkles, the patient hieroglyphics of the years.

"Did you know the narks have a twenty-four-hour tail on Ransom? 'Cause of all the co-caine over here?"

"No. I'm not surprised, though."

"They won't find it on him. They may find it on Mr. Clean's main man, Sprinter McGaw. Ransom's in hot cars and pills. Sprinter's selling the co-caine. Right under his nose."

Cool hitched closer. "Listening to every word, old timer."

"Turk knows he can't make a move without being watched. He's all steamed up. And worried. So tell him you can take the heat off him. If he leaves you be."

"How'm I going to do that?"

Sipping a little beer, Breathing Man smacked his lips. "Know Sham Shamberger, president of the Eight-Balls? In the White Fence family, across The Wash?"

"To say hello to, that's all."

Shamberger carried a black eight-ball, and was said to be able to throw it twenty feet and drop a man like a steer. He had no business over here in Chain Gang country, but Cool had actually seen him brazenly shooting pool in the Pastime. In fact, Sham sometimes played pool with Sprinter himself, with Sprinter acting like it was just a friendly game.

"Shamberger brings the co-caine in, hands it off to Sprinter!"

"How do you know?"

"Seen it happen. More'n once. Sham playing pool with Sprinter and a couple of dudes, showing that he's cool. Not afraid of nobody. Seen him sink the eight-ball. Sham picks it up out of the tray, puts it on the table. Only it ain't the same ball, Cool! I've seen him switch it with one he had in his jacket pocket. Now he's got the ball Sham brought, see?"

Cool shifted his weight. Was the old man dreaming? Making it up?

"Now he's got the ball, only it's a screw-apart ball and it's full of dope! Seen it happen. Time and again."

Cool stood up and moved around, chewing on it. It could be true! Screw-apart pool balls. Dope coming in, right under people's noses. Breathing Man beckoned him back.

"Tell Turk you'll give him a lead if he promises to leave you alone. He could pass it along to the narks and make points with them. They'd set a watch on Sprinter and grab him right here. And that would take heat off Turk."

Finally Cool said, "It's a long shot, but I'll drop it in his bucket and see what happens."

"Use the phone book in the Rescue Mission around the corner. Too many big ears in the Pastime."

CHAPTER

5

Just around the corner, on Spruce Street, was the In Jesus Name Amen Rescue Mission. No beds or meals were offered. The Mission was merely a snug harbor where down-and-outers could play checkers, cards, and dominoes, watch television, take a shower, dust off with lice powder, and store baggage and parcels.

When Cool entered, a desultory trade in stolen shoes was going on under the stairs in the rear. The stairs mounted to the balcony where baggage was stored. The shoes were stolen from drunks and were sold for money to buy wine to get other men drunk. Although twenty or thirty men were using the room, it was as quiet as a church.

At a counter on the right, Matt Campion, the director, was talking to a middle-aged man who was wriggling like a belly-dancer as they conversed. Matt had given him a New Testament the size of a deck of cards, and now they were discussing a packet of vermin powder he had tossed onto the counter.

"Will it really get the bugs?" the down-and-outer asked anxiously, scratching under his ribs.

"It'll get the live ones," Matt yawned. "Shower's free, but a towel's a dime."

The man paid and shuffled off to the showers.

Cool moved in. "What about the dead ones?" he asked the director.

"He ain't got lice, Cool, he's got the wine-itch. What can I do you for, Champ?"

"Just wanted to use the phone."

Matt started to lift a telephone from beneath the counter, but Cool shook his head. "Thanks, but this is a very heavy call. I'll use the phone booth."

"Tell your fox Matt says hello," said the director.

Cool flipped a dime with his thumbnail, glancing over the big, quiet room. Men studied their cards and added up spots on their dominoes. No one spoke; even the television set was tuned down to a whisper. "Don't you ever have fights in here, Matt? All these screwed-up old guys?"

"Never. They've had all the fight knocked out of them by the time they reach the Mission," Matt said.

Near the front door stood an archaic wooden telephone booth. The door squalled as Cool locked himself in. He dropped a dime in the slot, but hesitated before dialing, getting his thoughts together. At last he dialed Brother Marvin's Card Room. When a familiar, slow voice answered, Cool cupped his hand around the mouthpiece.

"Got a deal to offer you, Turk," he murmured.

"Speak up, Monkey, I can't hear you."

"I can't say this too loud, Turk. I'll take the narks off your tail if you let me stay out."

"How you going to do that?"

"Leave it to me. It's all set."

"Hey, wait! You been talking to the po-lice?"

"No, man. But I'm going to tell you something that

25

will surprise you. And all you got to do is set back and let stuff happen."

Sounds of voices in the background, as Turk muttered to a companion. A beer can cracked open; a girl squealed. Turk said guardedly: "Well, I might give you a chance. But first you got to come into the club as a standby."

Cool sighed. Take what you can get, he decided; hope for the best. "How's that?"

"Like I said. You join the Businessmen. But first you got to prove you with me. I got a man that needs a piece. There's an old German pistol in the window of the Cloverleaf hock shop on Logan Avenue. Bring it to me tomorrow at the card room."

Cool dug his thumbnail into the scarred wood of the door jamb. "You're talking about over a hundred bucks, Turk. I ain't got it."

"Man, you is so dumb! You buys it on credit."

"I ain't got credit, either."

Turk chuckled mellowly. "There's credit cards on every building site in town, Monkey. They're shaped like bricks. You throws your credit card through the window and checks out the merchandise. Hit it about twelve o'clock tonight. The po-lice are changing watch, and half the pigs is at the station house sucking up coffee and briefing the next watch on what's happening."

"But—"

"Hankins," Turk rapped impatiently, "I ain't got time to listen to you recite the Boy Scout's oath."

The dial tone drilled at his eardrum. Cool grimaced and kicked the door open. He groaned. Never get out of this thing. Up to his eyeballs in rattlesnakes. Sitting there, his gaze was attracted by the sight of Breathing Man entering the Mission, burdened by an enormous suitcase and a couple of cartons tied with string. He looked very proud of himself. Behind him came a slender giant also carrying suitcases. The sight of this stranger made Cool raise his head.

Hey, what's Breathing Man got hold of? The Grand Master of a lodge, or an African delegate to the United Nations?

For the stranger, slender as a rope and at least six feet five, wore black trousers with a yellow sash for a belt, a short red jacket, and a red fez with a black tassel. He had a trimmed, oval-shaped beard, and was smiling pleasantly.

Cool saw Matt Campion glance up from his mail-sorting. After first appearing impressed, he followed up his slack-jawed stare with a scowl that said,

I've been conned by experts, brother. Don't waste your time.

Cool walked over near the desk. He had to hear what was going on.

"Matt, this is Mr. Joshua Smith Kinsman," said Breathing Man. "He just got here from Africa."

Matt glowered at the mail and went on sorting. "Think of that," he said. "What can I do for you, Reverend?"

The stranger's voice was good-humored and rich. "I'm not a preacher, Mr. Campion. It's just 'mister.' "

He set down his valises and parcels to shake Matt's hand. Matt met his grip without enthusiasm.

"Mr. Kinsman has had. A rotten break," gasped Breathing Man. "Traveler's Aid gave him your address. For a flop and a couple of meals. I seen him get off the bus. And knew he was lost."

The bus from Africa? Cool wondered. He moved closer.

"Traveler's Aid better bring their file up to date. I don't have beds or meals anymore. You know that, Breathing Man."

"Don't you have a couple of cots up in the loft. For emergencies?"

"Not anymore. Health people closed me down. Some old boy hid an open can of sardines in his blankets, and I had an army of roaches in the place before I found it."

"I am not destitute, Mr. Campion," said the African. "In fact, I have ten thousand dollars in Tulami traveler's checks. The local banks refuse to honor them. Tulami, as you may know, is in West Africa—"

"No. I didn't know." Bored, the director glanced at the checks. On the face of the top one, a robin's-egg blue, Cool saw a lifelike design of a golden bee seated upon an old-fashioned conical hive. Matt shoved the checks back at the African.

"Sorry, Smith. Wish I could help, but—"

"It's Kinsman—Joshua Smith Kinsman."

"Right. Well, I'll bounce for a towel and a free shower, Smith, but that's about it."

Cool winced in annoyance. Why, this man might be the King of Tulami! Yet Matt treated him like a wino trying to hustle a bottle of Ripple. He thought of inviting him to stay at the foster home but realized it was a foolish idea. A king, perhaps, flop in the same pad with Marvin?

Matt dug up a towel from a bin below the counter.

"Thank you," said the African. "A shower will be most welcome."

"I'll call a friend at the Union Rescue Mission," said Matt, grudgingly. "They've got beds, and they'll give you meal tickets for odd jobs."

Cool shuddered. Cleaning toilets! Swamping mossy

showers! Meal tickets for white spaghetti and day-old doughnuts. His head swam. For suddenly his heart had become like one of those hollow Easter eggs with a window in one end through which you peered in at a vision of heaven. And in some secret way he knew that the African symbolized a way of life in a place more lovely than any he had ever dreamed of. That somehow Fate was bringing the two of them together so that he could help Kinsman and Kinsman could help him.

In a burst of joy, he tapped the man on the shoulder. The African gazed at him, and finally smiled encouragingly. Cool had the spooky feeling that the man's penetrating glance was revealing to him the very pattern of his soul, so that he saw him as if X-rayed, all his problems and ambitions perfectly drawn.

"I—I'm Walter Hankins, Mr. Kinsman. Here's seven bucks I'll loan you."

Cool heard Matt groan. Kinsman hesitated, then accepted the five and two ones Cool was offering him.

"That's very kind, Mr. Hankins. I don't know what to say."

"Say, thanks, brother. And so long," Matt grumbled. But Breathing Man was making panting sounds and finally blurted:

"Mr. Kinsman! Where I lives. There's a lot of room. And you can board with me. . . ."

And he described the big underground storm drain where he camped during the dry months. It was quiet and cool, there was clean silt on the floor, shade plants stood in tubs, and friendly sewer cats patroled the tunnels to scare off rats. Cool was embarrassed for him. Because any way you cut it, it was still a sewer, and Kinsman was certainly accustomed to the best.

But the African said he would be honored! He said

he would buy a sleeping mat that afternoon. He asked
Matt if he could store some things with him. The director leaned across the counter to study them. There were
several suitcases, a carton, a walnut box, and a big red
leather book.

"No food? Okey doke. Want to help carry them up to
the loft, Cool?"

Cool took the suitcases Kinsman pointed out and
climbed the stairs to the balcony, telling himself, *I have
just dived into something that will change my life!*

It was a faint hope, he knew. But when you lost hope
you might as well hang up your gloves.

CHAPTER

In the hot, musty stillness of the loft, Kinsman waited for Cool to pick a spot for his gear. Cool set the bags and boxes near a staircase leading to the roof. As he did so, he seemed to hear a sound coming from the wooden case. It was buzzing!

The African squeezed his arm. "Can I trust you, Mr. Cool?"

"Sure. It's just Cool, not 'Mister' Cool."

"What sounds like bees in the case is just that! Inside the case is a glass demonstration-hive."

Cool looked the case over. Screwed to the top of it was a golden emblem in the shape of a bee.

"The humming means that the bees are anxious to be about their work of seeking nectar and water."

"Oh."

Kinsman gazed down onto the big, quiet room, then peered earnestly at Cool. "The question is, where can the hive be placed so that the bees can come and go at will?"

Cool tried the door near which he had set the bags.

"How about the roof? I was up there once, helping Matt to tar a leak."

"Is there shade?"

"There's a ventilator. Used to go to a Chinese restaurant. I could put it there."

Kinsman beamed. "Fine. I'm placing the bees in your keeping. Until I leave for Washington, you'll wear this ring."

He twisted a golden, bee-shaped ring from his finger. ". . . It represents a queen bee. Queens are larger than workers, but cannot feed themselves or gather nectar. Yet only they can lay the eggs which produce drones and workers. There are many mysteries about the queens and the other bees' fierce loyalty to them. There is even a mystery about this bee ring!"

He pressed a hidden catch, and the golden queen, hinged to the ring itself, swung aside to reveal a small brass key lying in a slot like a corpse in a coffin. He reclosed it and gave Cool the ring.

"The key unlocks the hive case. Place the hive in the ventilator and bring the case back. Quickly! The hive must remain our secret."

Cool unlatched a door and stepped onto the tarred and graveled roof. There were pipes, a rusty tank on stilts, television antennas, and a vent curved like a ship's ventilator. Cool remembered when it had drawn up grease-smoke from a now-defunct Chinese restaurant and belched it out into the air.

He chewed his lip as he prepared to unlock the case. In the first place, he hated bees. In the second, things were happening too fast!

Who was this strange man? What kind of country was Tulami? Was it Harlem, perhaps, and Kinsman a hustler? Well, there was nothing much to lose. Cool turned the key in the lock. He removed the padlock and lifted off the top of the case.

Within, he found a gleaming, glass-and-brass beehive. He gazed in wonder at the activity inside it. Over white wax combs, most of them empty, crawled hundreds of small golden bees. Seeming to respond to the sunlight, swarms of them immediately began crawling toward an open slot at the hive's base.

Cool backed off. In seconds, a cloud of shining insects had risen like a flurry of golden snowflakes. With a musical humming they soared about the roof, as if testing the air currents. As more and more of them left the hive, a small fleet flew toward him, hovering about his head and hands. He grimaced and backed off. Some settled on the back of his hand, and he raised his free hand to swat them.

Yet something restrained him. For they seemed interested only in a ragged, inflamed cut between his thumb and index finger, which he had gashed when he piled out of his burning car last night. They covered it like a team of medics going into action.

As they moved over the puffy flesh, he felt a breeze from their wings. Faintly, he heard their singing. Their plump bodies were pure gold, without the honeybee's usual black stripes, and they were quite small.

As he watched, something happened: His wound grew numb!

He gazed at the hive. More and more bees were rising, like showers of tiny golden coins. They went streaming off toward some prize of nectar and pollen they could scent among the streets and alleys of Dogtown. The hive emptied quickly of workers, until nothing remained but drones occupied with mysterious chores.

When he looked at his hand once more, the bees had

vanished. A thin coating of wax glistened on his cut. It stretched when he flexed his fist; all the pain was gone.

Filled with wonder, he leaned inside the ventilator and saw two crossbars on which he could place the hive. From below, a breeze blew gently against his face. He placed the hive out of sight in the ventilator. The bees hummed about him. Though many landed briefly on him, none stung; he relocked the hive case and replaced the key in the ring, wondering what kind of bees these were, that healed cuts and did not sting. . . .

The African had one of his suitcases open and was laying out clean underwear and a folded shirt. Cool whispered,

"In like Flynn! And they treated a cut on my hand. What kind of bees are they?"

Kinsman winked at him. "All in good time, Brother Cool. You're so helpful, I'm tempted to ask you to guide me around town after my shower. I have lots to do, and I don't know the area."

Cool agreed. They went downstairs, Kinsman disappeared into the shower room. At the desk, Breathing Man was drawing up a shopping list on the back of an envelope.

"What you reckon he eats?" he asked. "Reckon I should burn a mess of greens and barbecue some ribs?"

Cool said that sounded good. "I'd bum a meal off you, but I've got to help Aunt Josie with dinner. We've got this new little devil, Marvin, that's a holy terror."

Presently Kinsman emerged from the shower looking neat and refreshed. He carried a small suitcase and two cartons. The top of one was screened, as though it might contain a live lizard or a snake. Cool took this carton, as Matt handed the African a slip of paper.

"This bank here will accept your checks for collection. Take about ten days, the man said."

"I'm grateful to you. Now, if you'd call me a cab, Brother Cool and I will be on our way."

Matt phoned, and a cab came. With a coffee-grinder transmission howl, the taxi roared off to the bank Matt had called. Kinsman left the red leather book on the seat when he went inside. Cool picked it up, wondering at its lightness. In fact, he had the feeling that it was hollow! He shook it, and something rattled inside.

So it was not a book, but a box that looked like a book!

"Nice-looking gentleman," said the cabbie. "A Shriner or some such?"

Cool glanced up and saw the curiosity in his eyes. "Don't know. I just met him. He's from Africa."

He rubbed the book's leather cover, which had the smooth resilient texture of live girl-hide. The book's title, *The Way,* was spelled out in raised golden letters. He rubbed them, and felt the *W* drop slightly under the pressure of his forefinger. Simultaneously, the cover loosened. He glanced up, saw that the cabbie was lighting a cigar, and peeked inside the box.

The first thing he saw was a collection of gold and silver medals with brightly colored ribbons. Also there was an envelope bearing the address:

The President
The White House
Washington, D.C. U.S.A.

Guiltily, he raised the envelope. Beneath it lay a packet of new currency. The top bill bore the portrait of Benjamin Franklin, and the denomination: $100. The packet was banded with a paper tape on which was printed:

$10,000.

He closed the box quickly and stared dazedly out the window at the bank. *I loaned him seven bucks, and he's got ten thousand. What goes on?*

CHAPTER

"Off we go!" exclaimed Kinsman happily, after returning to the cab. "I'll repay your seven dollars as soon as I get my money. But now I need a safe place to store this carton."

Cool directed the cabbie to a corner where, behind a green awning, there was a small grocery store. He did not trust most cabbies, who wouldn't know a secret if it were filed under S, so he was proceeding cautiously.

Am I being hustled? he wondered, as they got out. Sure I am. But what the heck, for seven dollars maybe I'm buying a part in a story Dogtown will never forget. Maybe I'll even get Turk's thumb off my windpipe for a while.

They got out; the taxi smoked away, and Cool led the way to the Greyhound bus station two blocks off. "Didn't want that dude knowing where we were going," he explained.

"A wise lad. I'll tell you a secret, Brother Cool: There are two dozen queen bees in this carton! The queens will soon go to the countryside, but in the meantime I want them to be safe, and to have a little air. You're thinking of a locker?"

"Right."

A *loony,* thought Cool. The bees not only looked like gold: Kinsman seemed to think they *were* gold.

In the station, the air was stale and overheated, heavy with the fumes of indigestible short-order cooking. An amplified voice was chanting something about a bus to San Diego. Cool led the way to the lockers.

"The ones with keys in them are empty," he explained. "Looks like there aren't any empties right now. No, there's one—" He swung a gray enameled door wide. The cubicle was empty except for one stale peanut.

"How's that?"

Kinsman fitted the box inside it. He opened the carton and began laying out rows of small wooden cases like oversized matchboxes. He set the red book in a corner. Cool took a queen case and looked it over. It was a plain block of soft wood with several round chambers drilled into it, the chambers being connected by passageways so that it resembled some sort of puzzle. Ordinary window-screening kept the bees from escaping.

"Notice the largest bee—that's the queen," Kinsman said. "The smaller ones are her attendants. They feed and tend her, because she can't feed herself."

Sure enough, a couple of smaller bees were stroking the queen as though she were a prize horse, while others nibbled at waxy plugs blocking a tunnel-like exit hole.

Kinsman talked while he worked. "The plugs are candy. If a queen were released in a hive, the other bees would kill her. But by the time the attendants have eaten through the candy, the hive has gotten used to her smell, and the bees accept her as their new queen. Then she gets busy laying the eggs that produce drones and workers."

Finished with stacking the cases, the African faced Cool with shining eyes, a noble figure in his red fez and uniform.

"At last!" he said. "So much planning! So much at stake!"

Cool's eyes shifted in embarrassment. He couldn't forget that Kinsman had his seven bucks, while there was ten thousand dollars in new bills in the locker. Nor could he keep from asking:

"At last what, Mr. Kinsman? What's at stake? The second coming?"

"In a way. America leads the world, and the bees will lead America. You'll understand before long. Lock the door and keep the key."

Cool pocketed the key, grinning feebly. Bad news, Hankins. Your hero is a loony!

They bought a straw mat, a flashlight, and some food for the African to take to Breathing Man's. Kinsman, vibrating with energy, moved fast, talking while he moved. He described his homeland.

He said the Republic of Tulami was only fifteen miles wide and fifty miles long, and had been created by the blunder of a surveyor named Gordon L. Tulami when the boundary between two larger nations was being straightened out after World War II.

He said that rather than fight over it, the other nations decided to let the strip stand as a buffer zone between their countries. And after all, there was little at stake but mountain hardwood groves, fruit trees, and villages bedecked with tropical flowers.

He said the country was a lovely jewel of emerald upland where two hundred inches of rain fell in the wet season. The people were healthy and handsome, and they sold the products of the soil and forests. But they needed industry and money, and so finally—

"—Finally," he said, becoming cautious, "I was sent on this mission."

"What mission?" Cool asked. He could see Tulami as if in a vision. Maybe it really existed. Maybe tropical fruit hung invitingly along the streets, and the rosewood girls were beautiful.

"In good time, I'll tell you," Kinsman said.

By the time they had finished their shopping, the sun was sinking into the jagged skyline of the city like a red-hot wrecking ball. They took a bus to the south end of the bridge across The Wash, where they got off. Cool pointed out a murky slot running down the center of the concrete riverbed. In the winter, he told the African, brown torrents of rainwater roared down that slot.

From their feet, a cement incline fell steeply, two hundred feet or more, like a ski slope. Rusty pipes studded it, and flights of steps were pressed into the concrete. The black mouths of storm drains yawned like mine entrances. Deep inside one of them, the Wildwood Lane drain, was Breathing Man's summer camp.

"Watch your step, now."

Cool led the way down a narrow flight of steps to a cross-ledge, his arms full of packages. The African followed, his red, yellow, and black garments glowing like the wings of a butterfly against the drab cement. Cool turned left on the ledge. In two minutes they reached a vast tunnel entrance from which a cool breeze flowed like water. Sniffing the breeze, Cool grinned.

"Smell that? He's got the ribs cooking. It's a pretty weird kind of pad, but it's cool and quiet."

They set out. A soft layer of silt carpeted the floor. In a short time they had left the sunlight, and Cool clicked on the flashlight they had bought. With his money, he recalled. It drilled a clean tube in the blackness.

"A lot of street people live down here, but mostly they stay in their own little side drains. Breathing Man likes the big one because it's got more dirt on the floor. Says it reminds him of the farm in Georgia."

The light flashed across old automobile tires half-buried in earth, a moldy doll, bottles choked with dirt, the black stains of old campfires. The tunnel was large enough to house a locomotive. They rounded a turn, and in the distance a spark of orange light burned like a lightning bug.

"There's his camp!" said Cool. "There's a street drain near it, and a faucet where he gets water. The fire is his barbecue."

They padded on. Cool wished he could recover his first impression of the African, that superstitious belief that the man was miraculously going to help him. Suddenly, Kinsman stopped. Cool stopped too, gazing at him.

"Is something wrong?" Kinsman asked gently.

"Well—okay, yeah."

Cool switched off the light. It was easier to rap in the dark. "Yeah. About the bread—my money. You borrowed seven dollars from me, but you have ten thousand. I looked in the book. I didn't mean to, but—"

"I'm glad you told me, Brother Cool. I borrowed the money because I need a faithful friend. And I don't know a better way to make a friend of someone than to let him help you. You helped me, and it made you feel good. And it told me that I could rely on you."

The paper bags crinkled in Cool's arms. The smell of barbecue sauce was stronger and sharper in his nostrils.

"That's true. But there's so much I don't dig about you, and in this town you only stay alive by being suspicious. I guess all your 'I'll-tell-you-later' jazz bothers me."

"Naturally. But soon you'll know the whole story. Until then, will you try to believe? Because soon I'll be helping you, as you helped me."

Cool studied the tall shadow beside him, and the bags rattled again as he switched on the light and offered his hand. "You got a deal, brother."

CHAPTER

Using an old paintbrush, Breathing Man swabbed the spareribs with a sharp red sauce. A tangy smoke drifted from the wheeled barbecue toward a drain in the ceiling. Gray light fell from it. Greens were bubbling in pans on the grill.

The old man had raked the silty floor. His property was defined by a half-circle of tropical plants growing in rusty cans and tubs. Many had dark-green leaves as large as canoe paddles. Sewer cats loafed everywhere, a kind of citizen militia against rodents. When Breathing Man sighed and let himself down in an officer's chair, a large calico tomcat quickly leaped onto his lap. Another cat had already taken over the African's lap-space.

"Cool," said Breathing Man, "why don't you? Open us some beers?"

Cool did, and they relaxed in a cool, dim silence like that of a church. Kinsman gazed in wonder at the camp. There was an Army cot against the wall, a footlocker, a folding table, and a small chest. Under a faucet in one wall sat a red plastic bucket. Near it, groceries were stored in a child's wagon.

It was all just as it had been a dozen times before when Cool had dined with the old man. But a little spider in his head kept weaving webs of worry for him. Kinsman—the bees—the money—and Turk. He sighed and stroked the marmalade-hued cat that had leaped onto his lap.

"Sure you can't stay for dinner?" asked Breathing Man.

"No, man. Thanks anyway. Got this mean little dude at the foster home. He'll be raising hell at dinner."

Kinsman looked interested. In the faint light from the street drain, his head turned toward Cool. "A disturbed child?" he asked.

"Rabies, is my guess. He's got to be the meanest kid, at age seven, in Dogtown."

Kinsman set down his cat and opened a carton. He lifted out two shiny gallon cans. "Honey," he said. Then he removed two cigar boxes bearing on their lids a red bee design. No doubt about it, Cool thought—the man was a bee-freak. Opening one of the boxes, he disclosed layers of slim, silver-wrapped cylinders about the size of pencil stubs.

"Honey candy," he said. "Give one of these to the lad before dinner. Let me know if it sweetens his disposition."

Cool could feel a softish tube inside the metal foil. He dropped the candy roll inside his shirt pocket, and when his eyes met Kinsman's he saw a secret mirth in them, like suppressed laughter. Presently, he downed the rest of his beer and stood up. He crumpled the can and fired it at a plastic bucket.

"By the way," he said. "I bombed on that call to Turk Ransom, Breathing Man. Zero."

"Pshaw," said Breathing Man.

44

"Turk Ransom!" said Joshua Kinsman. "Not the Turk Ransom with the Chain Gang?"

Cool stared at him, then at Breathing Man. "Dig this," he said to the old man. "He's only been in the city a few hours, but he's already heard of Turk."

Kinsman stroked the cat. "Did I tell you that I'm a professor of sociology? Probably not. I teach at the University of Tulami. We get all your big-city newspapers, and I've studied the Dogtown gang problem. In fact, I'm writing a paper on it."

Cool scratched his head. Not only a bee-freak, but now he knew about Turk. Well, maybe. And maybe he was on the gang detail and was sniffing around for a fink.

Cool decided to get careful.

He said, "Hey, so long, men," and started off down the tunnel.

Kinsman called after him. "If I'm not too inquisitive—what's your connection with Ransom?"

"None. Yet."

"Trust me!"

Cool halted. A sewer cat rubbed against his leg, another jumped to his shoulder. He wanted to confide. He still half-trusted him. He went back.

"He wants me in one of his gangs," he said.

"Take my advice: Stay out!"

Cool smiled. "You think that's bad? He's given me my first job: Steal a gun from the Cloverleaf hock shop."

His head told him to cool it, his mouth kept revealing his deepest secrets.

"Don't do it!"

"If I don't, they'll beat my head down to a stump. It's not like in the books, man. Turk's real, he ain't a case on page 154. Neither am I. At midnight I make up my mind. Well, so long, botha you!"

Kinsman rose and shouted after him. "I tell you it would be dangerous and unwise!"

Cool shouted back: "*I'll* tell *you* what's unwise: getting born in Dogtown!"

My brain's turning soft, he thought, abashed at what he had revealed.

When he reached home, darkness was settling on the hills and he was still pondering Joshua Smith Kinsman. He opened the door, wondering how much to tell his aunt.

Something like a hoop leaped from the floor and snapped tightly about his ankles. He fell flat, the piece of Tulami candy rolling from his pocket across the floor.

"Gonna hang you from a limb, you varmint!" screeched Marvin. "You done stole my cows for the last time!"

Wearing a cowboy hat that came down to his ears, the child swept up the piece of candy and ran for the stairs.

Cool lay there a moment, thinking, *Anybody can be dumb, Hankins.* He sat up and pulled a jump rope from his ankles: Marvin had tied it into a noose and waited for him to step inside. He looked up, and saw Marvin shed the candy wrapper as he disappeared up the stairwell.

Okay, Marvin! he thought. *So help me, I'll take you to the zoo in the morning and shove you through the bars of the gorilla cage. There's no living with you.*

". . . I met this fantastic dude today," said Cool at the dinner table. Marvin had not shown up, and there was an empty chair between Cool and his aunt. She was so busy keeping the peace among the hungry, talkative

46

children that only half her mind was on Cool. But Cool wanted to air the facts, to see if he could spot something he had missed before.

"He's skinny and wears a red jacket, black pants, and a red fez."

His aunt laughed. "Was he attached to a barrel organ by a little chain? Because it sounds to me like you're describing an organ-grinder's monkey. What did he want?"

"He wanted a crash pad and a guide. He's staying with Breathing Man. So I showed him around town."

"How much did he try to borrow?"

Cool scratched his head. She made it all sound like an ordinary Dogtown hustle. "Seven bucks," he muttered.

"And some poor idiot," said Aunt Josie, "will probably loan it to him!"

"Some idiot already did. It's hard to explain, see, but he's different. So I loaned him the money."

Aunt Josie raised her face to heaven. "Walter! As the Lord is my witness—!"

Just then a small figure appeared in the hall doorway. It was Marvin, smiling. A radiance seemed to emanate from him. The children noticed him and stopped eating. *Now what was he up to?* everyone wondered.

He wore a clean blue shirt, and was holding his hands raised as though planning to lay a blessing on them all.

"I washed my hands!" he exclaimed.

Aunt Josie did not appreciate being conned. She spoke coolly: "Very good, Marvin. Take your place, now."

Marvin trotted up and kissed her on the cheek. Aunt Josie sat openmouthed while he went to his chair. Suddenly, he dug in his pocket and laid three pennies beside Cool's place.

"I'm sorry I stole that candy, Uncle Cool," he said. "This is to buy you another piece."

"Man, you out of your mind?" Cool demanded indignantly.

"No, Uncle Cool. I just feel bad about what I done."

A little girl named Janet dropped her fork on the floor. Quickly, Marvin retrieved it for her. Janet flinched, but he laid it by her plate and returned to his own place. Cool stared at him.

Marvin ate with a good appetite, talking cheerfully with the other children. The big kids glanced at Cool and shook their heads. *He's sick,* they seemed to be warning. But Aunt Josie went to the kitchen, signaling Cool to follow.

"Didn't I tell you?" she whispered, beaming. "All that little old boy needed was lots of love, and something to eat besides French fries and cokes! We finally got through to him. It's like a miracle!"

"It's too much miracle for me," Cool said, wrinkling his nose. "Keep your guard up, old lady. He's getting ready to dump one on somebody. In fact, I'm going down to the Pastime Pool Parlor and shoot a few lines of pool, where I'll be safe."

From the stash place in his room, he got a couple of dollars, stuck his comb in his pocket, and started downstairs. On a bottom step he saw the silver candy wrapper. Some low voltage electricity trickled through his brain. The candy! He smoothed the foil on his palm. On the silver side of it was the design of a queen bee.

"Perhaps a piece of Tulami candy might sweeten his disposition," Kinsman had said.

Cool sniffed the paper, then licked it thoughtfully.

Was it possible? No, it was out of the question—that Kinsman was a drug pusher—that he had given Cool a spiked candy bar for the boy.

Yet, because he understood rotten little kids like Marvin so well, Cool suspected that there was something mysterious about the candy after all. . . .

CHAPTER

9

He shot some pool at the Pastime, drawing cheer from the brightly colored balls rolling and clacking in straight lines on the green turf of the tables—a hint of strict rules of order in a messed-up world. Through a fog of tobacco smoke, he saw the hands of a clock on the wall scissor off Hankins' last hour as a free man.

For now it was eleven-forty—time to hustle over to Logan Street. He left and plodded down grimy business districts, looped through a housing project, and reached a street of dark store fronts and sad hotels running east and west. A half-block away he saw the cold, frosty green of neon tubing—the show window of the Cloverleaf Loan Company. It stood at the intersection of an alley.

He moved on; the sidewalk was as lifeless as an old movie set. But plenty of action was hidden behind curtained bar entrances and one-night flophouses. Next to the pawn shop was a bar, its entrance draped; muffled sounds of music and loud noises came pumping through the curtain. He reached the hock shop and halted.

A nightlight webbed a sickroom illumination over the articles behind the glass. Turk had said the gun lay in plain sight. Cool prayed that it had been sold; but there it was.

Amid a litter of guitars, binoculars, knives, accordions, Japanese swords and cameras, lay an old German pistol, a red tag tied to its trigger guard. The display window was banded with the metal tapes of a burglar alarm. He knew that when the window shattered, a bell would begin to ring.

He could feel his heart beating like a bird rattling its wings against a window. *Okay, Hankins!* he asked himself. *Going to do it or not?*

Man, I don't know! Guess I do it. What else?

What with? No rocks around here.

He glanced into the alley. The dark canyon was lined with boxes and barrels. He hesitated, despising alleys. Cops rousted you out of them, muggers infested them. He saw a cat or a rat leap from an open barrel and scuttle into a clot of shadow. After the heist, he would have to run down this alley about two blocks, hide the gun in some weeds, and pick it up tomorrow.

Glancing up and down the street, he entered the alley and foraged along its edges for a bottle. On a barred window ledge he saw an empty pint wine bottle, placed there by some neat wino who did not believe in littering. He slipped it into his hip pocket, went back to the street and leaned against a light pole. He wiped his mouth. At last he pulled the bottle from his pocket, holding it by the neck like a German hand grenade. His big bee ring clinked on the glass.

He regarded the ring, scowling.

In Africa, the wearer of the bee would laugh in the face of a punk like Turk Ransom. But in Dogtown he was merely Walter Z. Hankins—Z for Zero.

He heard an engine purring, saw lights, and his head swiveled. He shoved the bottle under his arm. A car had entered the street. Headlights scalded the store fronts as a police cruiser rolled toward him, its tall antennas sniffing the night like an insect's feelers. He pressed closer to the pole, a mob of alibis colliding in his mind like thieves rushing for the back door.

"Well, see, Officer, I was just—I was—"

But the cruiser stole past on rubber-soled feet.

He sagged against the pole and moaned with relief. What if he'd hurled that bottle? He looked at it. It was only an empty Ripple bottle, but it would buy his way into jail as well as a stick of dynamite. And as he looked at it, his courage rushed together like drops of mercury, his will hardened, and he made up his mind.

He tossed up the bottle, caught it by the neck, walked into the alley, and fired it at a trash barrel. Bingo! Relief lifted him. He was out of it! For better or for worse! He turned back to the street, walking cockily.

But a sudden shout behind him rang up a clatter of echoes, and he froze.

"Hey, Monkey! Don't go 'way, man—"

A skinny shape under a cowboy hat stepped from a gap between two walls. Cool whirled and ran for the street.

CHAPTER

10

Other figures materialized from dark doorways and ranks of trash barrels. Still, he thought he might make it out; but a giant with the chest of a great ape was suddenly blocking the alley mouth. The street lamp gleamed on the shaven head of Mr. Clean.

Cool's brain computerized it and rapped out the answer:

Take one man, don't mess with a dozen.

He drove straight into the muscle-freak. Mr. Clean cocked something that looked like a Little League baseball bat. Cool plowed in, weaving his head, and as the Businessman swung, he stopped dead. He felt the wind of the bat on his ear; then he stepped in with a mean jab to the nose and a crushing uppercut to the jaw. He kept his fist lifting, as though the man were a side of beef and he was trying to hang him up on a hook. The top-heavy shape began to loosen like rotten scaffolding. Mr. Clean made a snoring sound and sat down.

But footfalls were closing in. Cool veered toward a trash can and swung it into the path of the first two men, drenching them in garbage and bottles. Down the alley a pistol flashed. A small-caliber explosion cracked. The bullet squalled off a brick wall.

"Young men!" a voice cried.

It sounded familiar, but Cool was too bent on escape to think about it. A wave of Businessmen was about to break over him. He hurled another trash barrel. Bottles and cans clashed and jangled on the paving, stopping three gang men in their tracks. Farther back, in the middle of the alley, Turk stood with his cowboy hat down on his face and his pistol leveled. It flashed and the bullet punched into the garbage can.

Cool turned to sprint for the street, bent double. But a very tall man was blocking the way, now, and the light from the street beamed on a red fez. His hands were raised, and in them Cool saw clusters of silver pencil-stubs. It was Kinsman, and he had brought offerings of candy!

"Young men!" he cried again. "Listen to me—!"

Cool collided with him and tried to wrestle him toward the street. "Get going, man!" he groaned. "They'll kill us!"

"Let us reason together!" cried Kinsman. "Let us eat together the sweet bread of brotherhood! From Africa I bring you—"

The sweet brother down the alley, Turk Ransom, fired at him. Cool heard Kinsman gasp and felt his body convulse. At the far end of the alley, shadows raced sidewise, then vanished as headlights flooded everything with chalky brilliance. An automobile swung into the passageway. A red dome-light began to revolve—a siren warbled. The Businessmen looked back, milled about for a moment, then came on toward Logan Street, their only avenue of escape.

54

Cool felt Kinsman sag in his arms. He lowered him to the pavement. Silver-wrapped candies rolled about the alley. Another police car swung in from Logan, so fast that it nailed them with its headlights and had to squeal to a stop. Both doors flew open. Twenty feet away, the other car braked. In the floodlit area between them a dozen Businessmen were trapped, as well as Cool, Kinsman, and Mr. Clean, face down in a welter of garbage.

But Turk had gone up a wall like a spider. A fire escape, lowered earlier, sheltered him as he dived over the parapet of the two-story building onto the flat roof.

Cars and cops seemed to spring out of the pavement. Two officers in gleaming caramel-colored helmets took charge with shotguns in their hands. "All right, punks—up against the wall!"

The Businessmen lined up, their hands raised. Sprinter McGaw, Mr. Clean's backup man, stood with a smile on his death's-head face. "But-but-but, Sergeant-sir," he stammered, "we was on the way home from the Boys Club, and—"

"And you were assaulted," the officer said. "Fine, Sprinter. We'll start from that basis and work backwards."

Cool knelt beside the African, who was trying to sit up. "No, no, man—lie still. Going to be okay. Be an ambulance here in a minute."

Kinsman heartened him by smiling. "Thank you, Brother Cool," he whispered.

From the rooftop, a cop called down:

"Hot dog! Got the big one up here, carrying a pistol and a sap! Let's go, Turkey—looking great there, buddy. Down the ladder, now."

Cool remembered that Breathing Man had said the

narks had a twenty-four-hour watch on Turk. Turk had walked right into it like a trusting child.

Later that night, at the police station, Cool remembered something funny. At the time, he had been too shocked to see much humor in it. Police cars had collected at the scene like flies on a dead dog, and officers were searching and handcuffing suspects, taking pictures, and writing things in notebooks. Joshua Smith Kinsman was lying quietly, perfectly conscious and assuring Cool that he was not going to die. The police were trying to unfold a collapsible stretcher.

Then, a car arrived with two tall aerials swaying, and two men got out of it, one of them the fat photographer who had taken Cool home last night. In the course of taking pictures, he spotted one of the silver-wrapped candies lying near Kinsman. He looked it over and called to one of the cops, a sergeant:

"Hey, Starkey! What's this?"

"Candy, I guess," the sergeant said. "There were some more of them in the Shriner's pockets."

They were calling Kinsman "the Shriner" now, because of his fez. Shriners belonged to some kind of lodge, Cool had heard, and the members all wore fezzes.

"Think it's safe to eat?" the fat photographer asked, unwrapping the candy.

"Safe or not, I'll bet you eat it, Tiff," the officer said.

". . . Delicious," said Tiff, munching the honey candy. "One more lousy thing I've got to avoid. What are you going to do with the candy you found in his pockets?" he asked Sergeant Starkey, running his tongue around his gums. "You don't need them for evidence, do you?"

"Evidence of what? They're in that plastic bag with his stuff. Help yourself."

The photographer ate three of the candies, pocketed a couple more, then grabbed a shot of Turk Ransom against the brick wall. "Thanks, Godfather," he said.

Turk glared in his direction.

Tiff asked Starkey: "Where are you taking the Shriner?"

"General."

"I'll ride along. Leo, pick me up at the hospital, will you?" he told the reporter. "I want some more shots of these guys before they lock them up."

"I'm entitled to a lawyer," Turk announced suddenly.

"You may even be entitled to seven-to-life, Turk," said an officer.

"Man, whattayou talking about?" Turk screeched. "That wasn't my gun, I found it on the roof! Man, this is ridiculous."

Cool asked the lieutenant who seemed to be in charge of things: "Can I go with Mr. Kinsman?"

"No, we need you as a witness. You can see him at the hospital tomorrow. Or the morgue. . . ."

The next time Cool saw the fat photographer was in the squad room at the police station. The room was large and battered, with brown flooring, a long oak table where officers were typing up reports, a few desks, and a rack of riot guns. The air was bitter with smoke. Typewriters clacked and phones jangled.

Detectives at scarred oak desks were questioning the Businessmen, who sat stony-faced in straight-backed chairs. Cool had been interrogated by Sergeant Starkey and the lieutenant, and he had told everything. The works. He might have denied all, but he was too angry to play it safe. Kinsman in the hospital, he didn't know how badly hurt. And Turk had tricked Cool—set him up for an ambush. The Luger in the hock shop was just bait.

Grimly he related the whole story, while the Businessmen listened with blank faces. Then he signed the statement Sergeant Starkey typed up with two fingers. His eyes went to Turk's face as he finished, but the leader's eyes were hidden behind the one-way mirrors of his glasses. But Cool read the message they were sending out:

You done tore it now, Monkey. Gonna gitcha, man.

A moment later, Tiffany waddled in. Cool watched him glance about, then go over and take a couple of pictures of Turk. The cop who was grilling Turk had a hamburger and some French fries in a basket. He wiped his mouth and grinned at the photographer.

"Want my fries, Tiff? Or the wrapper my hamburger came in? There's a lot of rich grease on it."

"No, thanks, Sanchez. I'm not hungry."

Sanchez gasped. "Hey, lieutenant!" he called, "Tiff ain't hungry! Write it down in the log. Another first for Cathedral Division!"

Tiffany smiled good-naturedly and joined Cool. "How you coming?"

"All right. Did you talk to the doctors at the hospital?"

"He's going to be okay. The bullet knocked out a little hunk of rib and shook him up some. They'll release him in the morning."

Cool let out a rasping sigh of relief.

"If you're through with this boy," the photographer told the lieutenant, "I'll give him a ride home."

"Might be a good idea," said the policeman, with a glance at Turk. "He is, to coin a phrase, a marked man."

Tiff took Cool's arm and guided him into the hall.

Outside, in the parking lot, a bitter mist was settling from the night sky. The photographer unlocked his car. As he got in, the little sedan groaned and tilted to the driver's side. He started the car, then sat there gripping the steering wheel with a serene expression.

"You know, I really feel fantastic," he said. "I haven't felt so good in years."

"Uh-huh," Cool said. He closed his eyes, exhausted. The long day, and the battle, had punctured something in him; and he was deflating like a balloon.

"In fact, I feel absolutely groovy," added Tiff. "I'm not even hungry! Isn't that amazing? By the way," he asked, "what does the Shriner do? He told me he's here on business, but he didn't say what kind."

"I don't know. I just met him this morning."

"I see." Tiff slipped the car into gear and finally headed up the street, following Cool's directions.

"That's a pretty classy ring you wear, Cool," he commented. "It looks like a bee of some kind."

"Yeah. I won it, uh, boxing."

"The famous Golden Bee award, eh? B for Bull. Funny, but I've never heard of it." He turned his fat face to Cool, grinning. Cool shrugged. "Have you eaten any of that candy of the Shriner's?" asked the newspaperman.

"No."

"You should try it. I've been wondering why I feel so good, and it just came to me that maybe it was something in those candies I ate."

A light flashed in Cool's head. "That's funny! Because—" He was thinking of Marvin again. But he realized suddenly this might be something Kinsman did not want broadcast, so he closed his mouth. Tranquilizer candy?

Tiff scrutinized him curiously. "What's funny, Cool? Come on—you're not leveling. Nobody's supposed to lie to fat men. Trust me, sport. What *about* the candy?"

Cool shifted on the seat. Actually, it was probably unimportant; and besides, the photographer had been very nice to him. Also, he needed influential friends. He said, offhandedly,

"Well, one of the kids at the foster home—one mean little dude—ate a piece of it. And it kind of settled him down. It was real peculiar."

"Sure enough?" Tiffany chewed his lip. "Huh. Another thing. How come you're wearing a bee ring, Cool, and there's bees on the wrappers of that candy? Isn't that a coincidence?"

"I guess Mr. Kinsman must like bees," Cool said.

"I guess he must. Because I don't believe in coincidences. I believe in things like inflation, baseball statistics, and stuff like that. And it's not just coincidence that Kinsman's hung up on bees, is it?"

"I don't know," Cool muttered.

Tiffany laughed and patted Cool's knee. "Okay. Forget it. I'll ask the Shriner. But listen—I hate to see you on the wrong side of a maniac like Turk. So if you need any help, call me at the paper. Here's my card."

"Thanks. You gave me one last night. It's that two-story house with the yellow car-body on the lawn."

"Right. Now listen, kid: Don't do anything without consulting me, okay? I mean anything involving Kinsman. I wonder if he's in *Who's Who*—? Hmmm. . . . Just thinking out loud. Man, there's a lot of energy in that candy! You wouldn't have any more of it?"

Cool smiled. "Nope. Thanks for the ride."

"I'll call you around eleven. I'm supposed to be off tomorrow, but I'd like to stay on this. . . ."

Watching the little sedan roll away, tilting like an overloaded rowboat, Cool realized he was on the story like a hound dog. He smelled something. In fact, so did Cool.

What was it about Kinsman and his funny-honey?

CHAPTER

11

In his sleep, Cool's mind floated like a child's lost balloon. A snake coiled about his throat. A leering, long-toothed man in a cowboy hat pointed a gun at him. A shark flopped up on a beach after him. Then a mosquito of sound drilled at his eardrum, and without waking he knew it was the telephone.

"Uncle Cool?"

He raised himself on one elbow and peered fuzzily at a small Chicana girl in the doorway. "What, Felicia?" he asked hoarsely.

"Telephone for you."

He waved her away and hunched up on the edge of the cot, drained like a broken crankcase. With sleep like that, who needed a disease? *Got to get out of this town! I have made a mortal enemy. Probably him calling me. No, he's in jail. Somebody calling for him. We're watching you, Monkey. You really tore it this time, man; you signed a statement.*

Wearily he pulled on a pair of red boxing shorts. Shirtless, barefoot, he padded down to the kitchen. Three of the bigger girls were making sandwiches for lunch. Aunt Josie would be at the laundromat. The girls had a transistor radio shrieking, so he stretched its cord into the dining room and closed the door.

"Uh-huh," he said, dully.

Panting. Heavy breathing. "Hello, there. Cool. . . ?"

"Breathing Man?"

"Yeah! You seen the paper? This morning?"

He was calling, he said, in excited little gasps and gurgles, for Joshua Kinsman, who had been released from the hospital this morning and had at once taken a cab to the pool hall, where Breathing Man had been on duty in the morning sun that nailed him to the wall like a golden spike. Breathing Man was calling now from the Rescue Mission.

Mr. Kinsman wanted to see him. Immediately. He wanted him to bring John Tiffany, whose name was on a story in the *Mirror-News* that said—and Breathing Man read the account aloud, syllable by syllable.

During a gang fight in the city's Dogtown district, Tiffany had written, a mysterious African political figure had been shot. He was not believed seriously wounded, and would probably be released this morning. At General Hospital, Kinsman had told the reporter of attempting to stop the fight by offering gifts of "brotherhood candy" to the gang members.

His nation, Tulami, was in West Africa. The nature of the candy he would not expand on. But reliable sources stated that it was concocted from honey and certain secret ingredients, and had a remarkably soothing effect on anxious persons. The story said that the candy had been used experimentally in work with disturbed youngsters.

". . . We're going back to my pad, now, Cool," said Breathing Man. "And wait for you. Don't bring anybody else. Just Tiffany. And be careful."

Cool said he'd have a cup of coffee and get going, but as he was pouring sugar in the cup the phone rang again. A high, wheezy voice said:

"Hi, kid! Quite a night, eh?"

"I was just going to call you, Tiff. Mr. Kinsman wants you to come to Breathing Man's pad."

He told him about the storm drain, then asked, "Are you a photographer or a reporter, Tiff?"

"I'm both. I have many gifts, Cool, one of which is that I'm such a slob that people in trouble will sometimes open up to me where they wouldn't to a young reporter in a sharp suit. I'll see you in fifteen minutes."

Carrying his coffee toward the stairs, Cool saw a man coming up the walk. He wore a gray suit, was gaunt and slightly stooped, and had long, limp gray hair. Under one arm he carried a clipboard. Cool's snap reaction was that he was a bill collector. The man rang the bell. The front door was open but the screen door was latched. Cool padded to the door and waited. They looked at each other. The man frowned at his clipboard.

"Walter Hankins?"

"That's me."

"I'm James Raynard, Walter. I'm an attorney, and I represent your friend, Sylvester Ransom." He had a sallow face, a long lean nose, and a habit of sucking a front tooth. *Slurp. Slurp.*

Cool sipped some coffee. "Sylvester, huh? That the same Ransom as Turk?"

"The same. I'll come in, if you don't mind."

"What for?"

"So we can talk more comfortably."

"I'm comfortable, man."

The man made a note on his clipboard like a shrink observing a patient. He sucked the front tooth again. "Suit yourself. I've been unable to arrange bail for Syl-

64

vester or any of your other friends in the Businessmen social club, and—"

"Knock it off about my friends. My friends don't jump me in alleys."

"Exactly what Sylvester wants to explain to you! He is distressed that you might think the altercation involved you in any way. The fact is, drugs have been coming into the area he, er, has a proprietary interest in, and he had a tip that someone was bringing in a quantity of cocaine last night. So he notified several of his associates that they must keep this from happening, by giving the person a severe scare—"

"And that's why he shot at me? And tried to kill Mr. Kinsman?"

Raynard picked out a point above Cool's head and peered at it.

"There is also the danger that young men loyal to Sylvester might become emotional about his plight and take action against you. He can't prevent this unless he is at liberty to contact all such persons and explain the situation to them." *Slurp.*

"If he's at liberty, he's liable to explain something to me, not them. I'd rather have him in jail."

"Sylvester wishes you to know that in the darkness he confused you with a member of the Picket Fence gang; and that in any case, he was firing over your head to frighten you."

Cool snorted.

"He feels he deserves a chance to explain matters to you. Visiting hours are until four o'clock at the jail. I believe I can secure the release of Frank Fuller—"

"Who?"

"You may know him as Mr. Clean. As well as others involved in the misunderstanding. But I'll need your cooperation to have a reasonable bond set on Sylvester.

You have been more than friendly in the past, he says, and if you'll visit the jail this afternoon—"

"So long," Cool said.

"I'll leave my card. Should you need legal advice, or want further explanation—"

Cool took the card he slipped through a tear in the screen door. He shook his head in disgust.

He took a shower, shaved, and combed his hair, with the feeling that he was aboard a truck roaring downhill with shot brakes. At the first turn, it was going to pile up in a tangle of metal, spinning wheels, and steaming wreckage; underneath it all would lie Walter Hankins. For in no way could he stay in town with Turk Ransom on his tail.

He socked his fist into his hand. He would get out! He would explain things again to Mr. Kinsman, who would certainly dig, by now, that you could no more reason with Turk than you could divide a fish dinner with a shark. And afterward—the wildest dream of his life!—maybe Kinsman would loan him the money for a ticket to Tulami, where he would start a new life!

Into a small suitcase of Aunt Josie's he stuffed a few clothes. From the stash place in his closet he drew out his life savings—twenty-seven dollars. He stood chewing his lip. A passport. Probably need a passport. Where did they sell them?

In the street, a horn honked. He looked down and saw a small blue car parked before the house. The fat photographer wallowed out of it. Cramming the last of a candy bar into his mouth, he started up the steps.

Cool shoved his suitcase under the bed and hurried to meet him.

Marvin met him first.

When Cool arrived downstairs, the seven year old was staring through the screen door at the photographer.

"Boy, are you fat!" Marvin crowed. He puffed out his cheeks and waddled around the entryway, showing Tiffany what he looked like.

"Out of here, punk!" Cool snarled, threatening to backhand him.

Marvin hissed, "You ain't so tough, sissy!" and ducked into the dining room.

"Any idea what this is about?" asked Tiffany, as they went down the walk. Kids were yelling as they played about the car body in the front yard, while others swung in old auto tires hung from tree branches.

"Not yet."

"Sure you don't have any more of that candy?"

"Nope. You've got a real sweet tooth, man."

"Oh, you've noticed?" Tiff opened the trunk of his car and pulled out a couple of cokes and some candy bars. He slipped a candy bar in the pocket of his brown-and-white seersucker jacket and handed Cool one. He offered him a soft drink also, then gulped down half a can without stopping. His plump pallid features gleamed as though waxed.

"Have to feed the wild animal that lives in my gut," he explained. "Let's go."

Near The Wash, Cool told him to park. "I hope you're a good hiker, because this is 'way up the drain."

"Do I look like one? I'd better have another coke before we take off."

He swilled down the soft drink in two tries, and belched. He picked up a heavy camera bag. "Vámonos," he said. "That's Spanish for, I wish I'd brought my skates."

CHAPTER

12

"Jeez, are you trying to *kill* me? You mean this is the only way into his pad? A sewer?"

Tiff moaned as he slid on his rump from one step to the next down the sheer face of the concrete embankment. Sweat glistened on his pale face and dripped from the loops of flesh below his chin.

"There's other ways, but this is the easiest."

Cool had elected to follow the photographer rather than lead him, so that he would not be crushed in case he fell. But as they reached the ledge, he scrambled past him and led the way.

He wondered what was on Kinsman's mind to call this meeting. Was he, after all, a missionary of some kind, come from Africa to bring salvation to the wild tribes of the United States of America? In that case, Cool hoped to persuade him that the cannibals of Dogtown would eat him raw if he made another ridiculous move like last night's.

The only possible salvation for both of them was to head for Tulami. And a vision of that lovely place shimmered like water in his mind.

At the mouth of the drain, Tiff took a picture of Cool leaning against the sidewall. He grabbed another couple of shots as they hiked on. They reached the gray light of the street drain and sniffed the smoke of frying hamburger. Kinsman came forward, neatly dressed and wearing his medals.

"Welcome!" he said. "Very good of you to come, sir."

Tiff absent-mindedly shook his hand, glancing about the camp. "Everything but dancing girls," he said. "What do you do when it rains?"

"I moves to a little room behind the Pastime Pool Parlor," said Breathing Man.

Panting, Tiff moved around. "Beautiful," he said. "No rent, and all the comforts. Say, reverend, you wouldn't have some more of that candy?"

Kinsman picked up one of the cigar boxes and opened it for the newsman. Tiff picked up a candy, then said, "How about two or three? I really had a fantastic high after the ones I ate last night."

"Take all you want. Eat two now and save the rest."

"Beautiful."

"Brother Cool, how about you?"

Cool took two of the candies and ate them as Tiff moved about taking pictures. Breathing Man tended the meat patties smoking on the grill. Tiffany fired off a flash shot of the African exhibiting the bullet hole in his jacket. He took a picture of Cool, Kinsman, and Breathing Man standing against the wall. Fifteen or twenty minutes passed. Breathing Man assembled hamburgers, and just as he was handing them around on paper plates, the photographer raised one finger for silence.

"It's starting!"

"What's starting?" Kinsman asked.

"The feeling! The groovy feeling." Tiff grinned at Cool. "Feel it?"

Now that he thought about it, Cool realized that the little spider that spun worry-webs in his brain had fallen asleep. He felt calm, yet exhilarated.

"I feel it! It's the honey, right?" he asked Kinsman.

Breathing Man handed Tiff a hamburger, but the photographer waved it away. "Not hungry. Thanks anyway." He stood there, a mound of happiness. "Men," he said, "I am not *hungry*. I am here to tell you that I could not eat a cream puff, a sirloin steak, or a candy bar. I am in a state of grace."

"It's a tranquilizer! Right?" Cool asked Kinsman. He felt as though he had just wakened on a spring morning with a cool breeze ruffling the curtains and the birds singing in the jacaranda tree. He could think of Turk Ransom without anger; could almost feel sorry for the punk.

"No, not a tranquilizer. An enzyme—a food substance found only in honey produced by the golden bees of Tulami."

"Are there any fat people in Tulami?" Tiff asked anxiously.

Kinsman chuckled. "None! In Tulami, no one has to eat his way to happiness. We are naturally happy. In two months, sir, your clothing will hang on you like an Arab's robes. You will lose at least a hundred pounds without experiencing hunger. Because your hunger is only a symptom of unhappiness."

Tiff eased himself into one of the canvas officer's chairs, which creaked dangerously as it received his weight. "And that's what you're going to do for the United States—? Open a string of fat-farms?"

Kinsman sat down also, and Cool sat in turn and started devouring his hamburger. Unlike Tiff, he was starved. The African picked up a small golden bowl and rubbed it with a polishing cloth. A design of bees crawled around the rim of it.

"No, no," he said. "I'm going to sell twenty-four queen bees to the United States for a million dollars a bee. My small nation needs money for a new medical wing at our university. Those bees will colonize hives all over your nation, and soon there will be Brotherhood honey for everyone. At that point the most profound social revolution in history will take place! There will be no more gang fights—no fights of any kind—less mental illness—"

Tiff started scribbling on a fold of newsprint. Cool was startled. Was Kinsman crazy, or not? Yet there sat John Tiffany, ignoring a hamburger and feeling groovy. And in Cool's own breast he felt a sort of music, like the last thrumming vibration of a harp string. Clearly, magic was taking place.

Breathing Man waved his hamburger in excitement. "That's beautiful, Mr. Kinsman! Only it ain't true, is it? How can it be? There's always been fightin' and sorrow. Hasn't there?"

"Not in Tulami, my friend. We have only twenty-six lawyers, because our arguments seldom go to court. We have so little mental illness that our only psychologist works part time as a magician at fairs. We have no army, few policemen, little illness, since most illness is the product of unhappiness."

Tiff looked up from his writing, his face keen. "Okay, brother; I believe you. My head tells me you're nuts, but my heart tells me to believe you. But who's going to believe you enough to pay a million dollars a bee?"

"That's the trick. That's it. And that is why I came to Dogtown before going to Washington, D.C. I want to prove that the fighting gangs of this city can be tamed!

That instead of fighting, and using drugs, young men can be persuaded to shake hands, seek jobs, and enroll in schools. Do you see the point?" he asked anxiously, peering around at the others.

"By using Dogtown as an experimental laboratory, I'm going to prove that violence can be eliminated. After Dogtown, I will tackle the United States. After the United States, the world!"

Cool closed his eyes to squeeze back the tears. It was beautiful. But it was a dream. Joshua Smith Kinsman was a man with a dream, and there were places in this world where dreams died. Dogtown was one of them.

CHAPTER

13

Cool wiped the hamburger grease from his hands on his jeans. It was quiet in the tunnel. Everyone was grinding on this news of the African's. He hesitated, then asked:

"Was getting shot last night part of your experiment?"

"I underrated Ransom's viciousness," Kinsman admitted. "I went to the pawn shop to try to persuade him to eat some of the honey. But I got the cart before the horse. First the honey, then the persuasion."

"How are you going to get the message to all the other gang-freaks?" asked Tiffany.

"By holding a Tulami Brotherhood ceremony—right here. This bowl will hold pure honey. Each participant will dip up a spoonful and eat it. Then we will talk business. The ceremony precedes all important work in Tulami."

"How come you didn't start by writing to the President?" asked Tiff.

"I did, but Tulami is tiny. I have a ten-minute appointment with the Vice President six months from now. So I came here to stage my experiment and make the authorities take me seriously."

"How are you going to get the gang dudes here?"

"With your help. I'd like the news broadcast in the press and on television. If necessary, the police may have to bring some of the boys."

"I'll pull Lieutenant Rock's sleeve—he heads the gang detail. —Look," Tiff said, "if this has been going on in Tulami for so long, why didn't you make your play before?"

"We took peace for granted. We assumed that our serenity was inborn. Then a scientist seeking new uses for honey—one of our few marketable products—discovered that the honey is rich in the mysterious enzyme I mentioned. His work with vicious rats convinced us. The key ingredient is not really a drug, but a food substance that remedies some lack in the human brain."

Tiffany suddenly struggled to his feet. "Okay! Okay! Feeling the way I do, I've got to believe you. I'll play along, if only because all two hundred and seventy pounds of me demands it. So spell it out for me and I'll get things rolling."

Kinsman said it would start with a peace parley at ten tomorrow morning. He wanted the most influential gang leaders in the city to take part in it. They would hear his story, discuss his plans, and he would issue rations of honey to each gang leader.

"Got enough honey?"

"Enough to start. If the leaders and their lieutenants are with us, the rest will follow. Cool is taking care of a small working hive for me where more honey is being manufactured. In Tulami, we have hardly enough for our own needs."

74

"How about Turk?" asked Cool. "You want him at the meeting?"

"Mr. Clean can represent him. I'm afraid Turk will need special handling before he can be useful—some honey sneaked into his diet, perhaps."

"I'm supposed to visit him at the jail," Cool said. "I'll bounce the idea off him and see what he says."

"In the meantime, there is a small blue bag in my valise at the Mission. Will you get it and bring it to me tomorrow?"

Cool said he would. Tiffany was already scribbling notes for his story. "Let's go," he said suddenly.

After the climb back up the concrete steps in the roasting heat, Cool thought the photographer was going to collapse. He sat in the newspaper cruiser and panted.

"Can I get you a coke out of the trunk?" asked Cool.

"No, thanks, sport. Not thirsty. Isn't that a laugh? I'm not thirsty! I'm not hungry. The ants in my arteries are asleep. —Okay," he sighed. "What's first?"

"The Mission. I'll get that blue bag. Then I've got to visit Turk at Central Jail."

A white Continental was parked before the In Jesus Name Amen Rescue Mission, and Tiff pulled up behind it. A vanity license plate read: ABCDEF. As Cool got out, Tiff growled:

"What kind of damn fool would pay twenty-five dollars to spell the alphabet on his plates?"

"Maybe a kindergarten teacher."

"Kindergarten teachers don't drive Continentals. Okay, hurry it up."

Bouncing on the balls of his feet, Cool entered the Mission. Matt was explaining to a man how to use the delousing powder, as Cool swung by the desk. "Just going up to get something for Mr. Kinsman," he said. Matt nodded and he climbed the stairs to the balcony. Near the top he halted in shock.

A stranger was pawing through Mr. Kinsman's bags.

He resembled any middle-aged man in a gray suit tailored to fit a small paunch, with a florid face and a receding tide of turnip-colored hair. He was smiling vacantly as he examined the walnut hive case with the bee handle screwed to it. Cool heard him humming to himself. He turned suddenly and looked at Cool, but continued smiling.

"Oh, hello, there," he said.

"Hello." Cool climbed the last couple of steps. He ignored the man and started moving suitcases around.

"Do you work here?" asked the man.

"Yes, sir. Part time. Have you got something stored here?"

"No. Excuse me—what are you doing?"

"Routine roach-check. Can I help you?"

"Oh, no, thanks." The stranger glanced down at the derelict men below. "Sometimes I come here to look at those poor men and just wish that I could help them. I'm a vitamin manufacturer. I tried to interest the Government in a massive program to supply vitamins to the poor. You see, all that ails them is a lack of proper nutrition. But they turned me down. So sad, because it would have met the needs of so many people. . . ."

Yours, too, thought Cool. *For money.*

The stranger offered Cool a flat brown lozenge. "Have one? It's chewable Vitamin C."

"No, thanks. Just brushed my teeth."

"Well, I must go. By the way, my name is Parsons. Read this little brochure when you have time." It was printed in green ink on slick paper.

76

Cool glanced at the title. "INTESTINAL FAILURE: Commie Plot?" it read. "If all Americans ate only one quart of my yoghurt daily, plus a dozen vitamin tablets, say Famous Nutritional Experts, their moral and patriotic well-being, as well as the health of their lower bowel—"

He watched the man reach the floor and leave. *There's a cat that reads the papers,* he thought. Parsons had read about Mr. Kinsman and followed the bait here—the magic food supplement Tiff had written about. For it was not pity for mankind Parsons was high on: He was wild with greed.

In the suitcase, Cool found a blue velvet jeweler's bag under some shirts. He relocked it, checked out the hive on the roof, and ran back to the car. The Continental was gone, and Tiff was looking at a paper on which he had scribbled something.

"His name is Parsons," he said. "I called the city desk and checked out his license number. The car is registered to Parsons Natural Foods Corporation. What's he doing here? Selling yeast tablets to bums?"

"He was sniffing around Mr. Kinsman's stuff. He's wired in to stuff like magic candy, and when you wrote about it you said you'd met Mr. Kinsman here."

"You got it, kid. There's going to be a lot of people interested in this. Maybe you'd better move that hive."

"I'm going to. Tonight."

The car was moving. "Where?" Tiff asked. "That's going to be a hard thing to hide."

"Don't know yet. My mind's kind of floating—"

As they were passing over The Wash, Cool glanced down at the strict geometry of the railroad yards, and gave a start. "There!" he said.

"Where?"

77

"See that line of old cabooses? I'm going to hide it in the doghouse on top of one of them tonight. I'll open a window so they can come and go."

The perfect place! And somehow his mind had flipped out a card that said, *Caboose—remember?* without his having to think about it. So the honey also gave you the smarts.

"I'll drive you over after I finish up tonight."

CHAPTER

Upstairs were the cells, a men's block and a women's. Sometimes prisoners yelled rude things down at passers-by. The jail was near the downtown area, just off a grimy little park. Downstairs were the business offices, mugging rooms, and a long room where relatives visited prisoners.

Cool came in off the street and saw a long, narrow room like a wide hall, with a green tile floor and chairs against one wall, occupied by people waiting to visit prisoners. There were old people, young people, men, women, and children. All except the children were smoking and looking disconsolate. Typewriters clattered behind a partition.

A door opened and a man came out. He looked familiar. His hair was long, the color and texture of an animal pelt, and his nose was long; and as Cool studied him, the man sucked a front tooth. It was Turk's lawyer.

Raynard quickly spotted Cool and came straight to him. He began opening a black briefcase about as thick as a cheese sandwich.

"Good! Good!" he said, with a twisted smile. "Appreciate your coming. So you're going to cooperate. Fine. I have a couple of papers here, one for Sylvester Ransom, one for Frank Fuller. If you'll sign them—they're just standard forms—I think I can secure the release of both your friends immediately."

"And then my standard friends can start beating on my standard head, right?"

Raynard moved closer and pushed the papers at him. "It's pointless to talk that way, because—"

"It's pointless to talk, period."

Raynard was silent for a moment, peering at him tight-lipped. "So what do you plan to do?"

"Okay, man, that's better. Show some respect. *My* lawyer says don't sign anything, but tell the police I'm not pressing charges against Mr. Clean. They'll let him loose. Then at nine o'clock tomorrow morning, a couple of cops will pick him up at his pad and take him to a meeting we're holding."

Raynard's eyes filmed over with distrust and he backed up a step. "What are you trying to tell me? What are you talking about? Where do the police come into it?"

"If he's there, and comes along okay, we'll let Turk out in a couple of days, too. If he's not, Turk's up against assault with intent, possession of a concealed and unregistered firearm, conspiracy—"

"Knock off the crap," said the lawyer. "What's the bottom line?"

"We're holding a meeting, and we want Mr. Clean there. Depending on what we work out, Turk gets out on bail, or he doesn't. It's up to him and some other dudes. That simple."

"What other dudes?"

Cool smiled and looked at his ring. "Oh, well, you wouldn't know them. Sham Shamberger, Obie Valenzuela, Bread Williams, Indian Red Morales—"

The lawyer's hand made a waxing gesture. "The hell I don't! They're all, er, rivals of Ransom's." *Slurp.* "I'm against it, but as long as you're here why not talk to him? In the meantime, I'll notify the jailer that you have no objection to Frank Fuller's being released."

"He better be there tomorrow morning, or there'll be a capias out on him."

The lawyer sneered. "Where'd you hear of a capias?"

"My lawyer. It's a paper that says, *Pick him up.*"

"Tell your lawyer, who I presume is a fat newspaper photographer named Tiffany, that practicing law without a license is an offense punishable by— Oh, hell. Go to the window and sign the book. They'll bring Ransom down. Maybe he can explain things to you so you'll understand."

When they called his name, Cool went into another room with a line of windows in an inside wall. Before each window a straight-back chair was bolted to the floor. On a ledge beneath the windows were ash trays and telephones, one per window. On the other side of the window were other telephones, where prisoners sat holding hand-sets, looking as though they had long-distance calls, though the callers were only a foot or two away.

He sat where they told him, and soon an officer brought a tall, skinny young man with a six-hair goatee, long eyelids, and long teeth. Cool hardly knew Turk in his jail blues—dark blue pants, light blue shirt. He had been stripped of the spurious look of elegance bestowed by his street threads. Playing it cool, he drew on a cigarette before picking up his telephone, but in his murky eyes Cool saw hope swirling like oil on water. Turk had done a lot of time, and could do a great deal more if somebody didn't lift the rock off his back.

He crushed the butt in a plastic ash tray and took his time about picking up the phone. Then he said, looking into Cool's eyes,

"Yeah, hello, Monkey. What's happening?"

"We have a long-distance collect call for you, Sylvester," Cool said. "Will you accept the charges?"

"Cut the bull," said Turk. "Did you talk to my lawyer?"

"Yes, sir. Told him no."

"No what? I don't dig."

"No day, no way. The man's still preferring charges."

Turk's bulging eyes veiled themselves like a bird's about to fall asleep. He glanced up and down the line of disconsolate blue-clad prisoners. He leaned toward the glass.

"Look, uh, I wonder if we understand each other, man. It's hard to talk this way, and you probably don't dig what I'm saying. This misunderstanding about what's-his-name—we got to clear that up. Everybody's sorry, and people that aren't now will be later. You ever been in Folsom Prison?"

"Not that I recall."

"Well, I have. It's a, you know, hard-time place, and the hardest section was called Adjustment, where you went if you had a misunderstanding with a guard. No talking between cells, no messages. So, see, we'd tear a thread out of the strong-sheet that we slept on, right on the floor, see, and tied it to a cockroach that we'd let crawl under the door and into the hall. Then the other guy tossed a thread with a cigarette on it across your thread and pulled it into his cell. The note, or junk, or

82

whatever was tied to the other end of your thread came right along."

"I've heard," Cool said. "So?"

"Man, I don't like talking into a tape recorder like this. Don't you righteously follow?"

"You don't want to go back to Folsom."

"Right. And they're talking about this mess-up being in violation of my parole about six ways. That's ridiculous. Because I like it so much better out here, where I can pass messages without a Western Union cockroach."

"Out here?" Cool said, looking about him. "Hey, which side of the glass you on?"

Turk shook another cigarette from a pack, put it between his lips but did not light it, having no matches.

"What did you bother coming down for?"

"To tell you about a meeting tomorrow. Eight heavy gang men are going to meet at Breathing Man's pad with Kinsman. Tomorrow peace is coming to this troubled town, Turk. No more cockroach messages and bad stuff happening in alleys. We want to get you involved, but the man says not yet. Not while you're all jived up. But keep the faith, and we'll have you out."

Turk ground the cigarette into the ash tray. "Hare Krishna, hare hare!" he said. "Piss on peace, Monkey. You are playing with half a deck upstairs. I would like to see the day eight heavy men sat down to a meeting."

"You will, Turk. I mean it, now—we're on your side. But other people have to be protected, too, so we're going to get set up first. Mr. Clean will be there talking for you. There's really going to be peace, the man says."

Turk stood up, looked at Cool with bitterness, and said, "You dumb bastard."

"Your three minutes are up," Cool said. "But your six

years aren't. Think about those cockroaches, Turk."

He figured he had nothing to lose by butting heads with him. Turk Ransom could not possibly despise him more than he did. But if Kinsman were talking straight, Turk would soon have no fangs to bite with.

If he weren't, then Cool Hankins was definitely going to buy a ticket some night soon and start traveling.

CHAPTER

15

The last of the young and old walking wounded were straggling dazedly from the Mission when Cool and John Tiffany arrived. Night had come on a warm breeze, though some rusty color still stained the sky, as though a mechanic had rubbed it with a rag. The men did not bunch up on the walk. Loners all, they drifted off to places where they could get a meal, a cot, or a doorway for the night. Cool knew places where they fed them plain spaghetti, laced with so much salt they sucked the water up like camels and so ate less. He wondered what the derelicts would do if they had some of that miracle honey in their diet. Get busy passing out handbills for a dollar an hour? Go back to jobs they had had before they slipped out of gear?

It was an experiment Mr. Kinsman would certainly want to make.

"Right back," Cool told Tiff.

He gave Matt a story about Mr. Kinsman needing one of his cases. Matt, turning off the lights, told him to hurry it up. Cool did, and was out like a burglar in three minutes with the hive case. It was heavy; bees were surprisingly heavy, sitting down. Tiff stored it in the trunk of his car.

At Cool's direction, he drove across the bridge, then cut back toward the railroad yards through a jungle of small, ancient factories. The firms made things like wire, bottle caps, batteries, and paint. Railroad tracks ran in to loading docks. Cool spotted the set of rails that led out to the area where the cabooses were parked.

"I'll walk from here."

The tracks led into a cavelike darkness. Red, green, and blue points of light floated in it like fireflies. The wind smelled like stale peanuts; then it swiveled to another smokestack and reeked of soap. He floated over a dead-black world of crushed rock. Far away, a freight train slipped past with muted clankings. Now a wall rose slowly from the earth as he approached, and he saw by the roof line that it was the string of cabooses.

Halting, he looked and listened for guards. Only a far-off surf sound of auto traffic, then a plane passing over. He decided to try the last caboose in line. Hurrying on, he reached the car, saw that it was blue-green. He hoisted the case onto the rear platform and clambered aboard; he tried the door—unlocked!

Inside, the air was stale and hot. There were bunks, a coal stove, and a couple of tables bolted to the floor. He moved around and found a ladder to the cupola upstairs. Climbing it one-handed was tricky, but he reached the small, glassed-in cabin. There was a table and a chair, nothing else.

He checked the windows. They could be pushed out from the bottom, and he opened one enough so that the bees could come and go without its being obvious. He opened his bee ring, removed the tiny key, unlocked the case, and set things up. It was too dark to see how the bees were taking it, but he patted the case.

"Get your rest, babies," he told the insects. "You'll be working for the U.S. Government next week."

CHAPTER

16

A cool dawn the color of orange sherbet woke Cool.
With a shock, he came awake.

It'll never work, he told himself anxiously.

*I was high on that candy. Eight heavy gang men sit
down and talk peace? Not this year, not even next.*

Shaving, he thought of letting his beard grow, buying
different clothes, hiding out at some crash pad for run-
aways. All the magic was stored away with the Chinese
rings and marked decks. Still, he had a date with Mr.
Kinsman, and had to go through with the farce. Then, if
they didn't both get killed in the brawl, maybe they
could buy two tickets to Tulami and flee the town.

Tiff showed up at nine-thirty and they drove off. The
photographer patted his belly.

"I've lost four pounds. It's beautiful!"

"Think you've lost enough weight to squeeze
through a street drain?" asked Cool. "We could save
ourselves that hike up the sewer if you could."

Tiff doubted it, but Cool directed him to a street
called Wildwood Lane, where big, dark, dusty magno-

lias stood baking in the hot morning. Their heavy, white blossoms looked like doves nestling in the dark-green foliage.

Suddenly, crossing an intersection, Tiff cried angrily: "What the hell is *that*?"

He was staring at a red panel-body truck parked at the curb a half-block farther on. Big black figure 8's were painted all over it. "Channel 8 news!" he piped, in the voice of an angry midget. "Who the hell invited *them*?"

"It was all in last night's paper, Tiff. You wrote that Mr. Kinsman was staying in a storm drain."

"But I didn't say which one! I'd have sold the story to the wire services and made a bundle. One of the lousy cops told them! Who else knows where Breathing Man lives?"

He stopped and glared down at the street drain. Electric cords trailed into it from the truck, and a man in the cab stared at them. "There is no way I can crawl through that drain," Tiff mourned. He raised his voice and shouted at the man in the truck, who wore head-phones: "Hey, what's going on?"

The man removed the headphones and said, "What?"

"What's happening?"

"Oh, some kind of conference. In a sewer—dig that! A lot of cops and kids have been crawling through that drain in the last half hour."

"We're gonna be late," Cool said.

Tiff gunned away, swearing.

From hundreds of feet away they could see the glare of lights in the storm drain. Tiff had traveled up the drain at a rolling gallop, frequently mopping his face on an enormous handkerchief. And now, Cool made out the camp, and a circle of people sitting on the sand. Others stood around. As they drew closer, Tiff snarled:

"Morrie Mays! That louse!"

Cool had seen Morrie Mays on the local television news, a tall, elegant, gray-haired man wearing a red coat with figure 8's on the lapels. Two other men in red coats were arranging lights. Tiff charged up to Mays, who wore tan powder-base.

"Who finked, Morrie?" he demanded.

Mays smiled calmly. "Why, no one, John. It was right there in your story last night. I just put the clues together and realized it could be nowhere but Station 32 of the Wildwood Lane storm drain."

"Gaah! You and Lieutenant Rock. I hope the Farmers put bib overalls on him next time he invades their turf."

Cool shot glances around. Lieutenant Rock was not there yet, but nearly everyone else was. On straw mats in a campfire circle on the floor sat seven young gang men, with seven cops behind them. Cats wandered about, and it amused him to see several curled up on the laps of the seated gang leaders and officers. The young men wore deadpan expressions. Most of them smoked nervously.

Mr. Clean was there in a black muscle shirt, staring with bitter hostility at Cool. And there was a Chicano boy, Obie Valenzuela, leader of the Batos Locos, who was small, with handsome features that masked a brain like a knife. There were others Cool did not know, but one he did know was not there: Indian Red Morales, of the Nighthawks, who would round out the Big Eight.

Joshua Kinsman sat on the cot beside Breathing Man. He rose presently and carried the golden bowl into the ring and placed it on the sand. Cigarette butts littered the ring. There was already a plastic bucket there, a roll of paper towels, a box of plastic spoons, and a carton for trash.

Bread Williams threw a cigarette butt down and asked: "What you going to do, man—make lemonade?"

"Something even better," Kinsman promised. He glanced at his wrist watch. "Lieutenant Rock should be here now. I'll explain as soon as he and Mr. Morales arrive. But in the meantime, please pass these candies around. There's one apiece."

A plate of African candy started around the circle. The cops sat behind the boys and watched. Then there was a rasping sound, as the gutter grating twenty feet down the tunnel was moved aside, and a big, blond man in a red golf shirt and blue-and-white checked pants started down the iron ladder bolted to the wall.

Behind him came a tall youth in a gold shirt and black pants, wearing a red headband. This was Indian Red Morales—and Cool knew the blond man was Lieutenant Rock of Juvenile Division. Morales ran the clubs in the Los Tres area around Third Street.

Lieutenant Rock took a cigar out of his mouth and looked the scene over. He looked more like a golf pro than a cop. He grinned.

"I had to see it!" he said. "I knew I'd see all you guys together in one place sometime, but I really thought it would be San Quentin. Don't get up, Fuller," he said, as Mr. Clean got to his feet. "I'm just folks."

"Sit down," the cop behind the muscle-freak said.

Mr. Clean threw his silver-wrapped tube of candy on the ground. "There's no law!" he said. "And I ain't eating any of that crap. When you let Turk out, then we can talk about a meeting."

"Didn't the officer explain the purpose of the meeting?" Kinsman asked him.

91

"Something about brotherhood," Mr. Clean snorted. "—Hankins, it's going to be between you and me, next time I see you. I hold you responsible."

"It was between you and me a couple of nights ago, baby," Cool said. "Come on, man—give it a chance."

"When I see Turk on the sidewalk, we'll start talking," the Businessman said. He headed for the ladder.

Rock waved back the officer as he started to follow him. "It's true," he said, "we can't hold him. He's got his rights, the louse."

The television cameraman hurried to grab a shot of the gang man climbing the ladder. Indian Red Morales, momentarily in the shadows, started toward the circle of mats; but suddenly there was a wild, cat-howling screech of pain. One of Breathing Man's cats streaked away into the darkness, as Morales swore and backed off.

"What the hell was that?"

"That was a cat, Red," said Lieutenant Rock. "Cats are a sewer dweller's best friend. You stepped on his tail."

"They ain't *my* best friends," Morales snarled. "My God, how many of them is there?" He peered around the camp.

Breathing Man picked up the cat Morales had stepped on. "There was fifteen," he said. "But another one came last night."

"That makes seventeen," said Bread Williams. "Counting Red."

Morales stared at the black youth, then cursed him. Williams started to his feet. But Lieutenant Rock's hand fell on his shoulder.

"All right, men," he said wearily. "Cool it, huh? As a favor to me? This is billed as a peace parley, not a gang rumble. Reverend," he said to Kinsman, "maybe you'd better get started on your sermon. Sit down, Red. As a favor, okay? Have a piece of candy."

"Move the damn cat," Indian Red growled. A black cat was curled up on the mat where he was supposed to sit. It was clear that he had a thing about cats. Breathing Man shuffled over and carried off the cat. Kinsman offered the gang leader a silver roll of candy. Morales looked it over, unwrapped it, sniffed it, and finally ate it, with a shrug.

Kinsman looked around. "I believe we're ready," he said.

CHAPTER

17

Kinsman explained that, while he discussed his plan, the boys could start the brotherhood ceremony. They did not have to believe in it, he said: it would work anyway. He asked them to wash their hands in the plastic bucket, dry them on the paper towels, place the towels in the carton beside the bucket, and help themselves to all the honey they liked from the golden bowl. Use a clean plastic spoon for each spoonful.

He performed the rite, himself, to demonstrate how it was done. Then, from the blue velvet sack Cool had brought from his suitcase at the Mission, he extracted seven gold rings and placed them on a plate beside the honey bowl.

"After we've finished our business, each of you will be given a ring to wear. To make you brothers, you see."

Somebody laughed. "Brothers!"

Cool sat beside Breathing Man, on the cot, and watched the young men go through the motions. Obie Valenzuela rinsed and dried his hands and dropped the

94

paper towels on the floor. Then he ate some honey. Indian Red balled and threw his towel at a cat. Sham Shamberger, Bread Williams, Louie Diaz, and Rance Coker of the Elegants splashed a little water, helped themselves to honey, and discarded their towels on the sand. Everyone seemed careful not to deposit a towel in the waste box.

And while they performed the rite, Kinsman stood outside the circle and talked quietly about Tulami, and the part the honey played in the nation's daily life.

"So we all going to be peace-freaks," Morales said.

"Brothers," muttered Valenzuela. "That would be the day, huh?"

Kinsman went on talking, his voice flowing cool and smooth as a brook. But Cool thought anxiously, *Get to the point, man–they won't sit still forever!* Then he realized that the African was waiting for the honey to take effect before he got down to the nitty gritty. The gang men listened because people liked to be told a story, and Kinsman was a storyteller. He made you hear the parrots in the trees, feel the cool water of the highland streams, and smell the sweet breath of the cup-of-gold blossoms.

Cool took note that the boys had stopped smoking.

Indian Red helped himself to some more honey. While he was up, he picked up from the sand a couple of discarded towels, and dropped them in the box. Cool sat up straighter. A small point. But he looked at his watch. It had now been twenty minutes since they ate the honey candy. He saw Kinsman's facial lines ease.

"Mr. Morales," he said, "why do you start fights?"

Scowling, Indian Red sat down again. "Man, *I* don't start fights! But I control my turf, and got to fight back sometimes."

"Lieutenant Rock tells me one of your gangs attacked the Jesters in Mr. Williams' area last month."

"Broke a man's arm and burned his car," said Williams, piously.

"You're talking about that dude, Rebel?" Morales retorted. "Rebel jumped one of my men the week before. That's why my men jumped him."

"You mean Jap Garcia? Rebel jumped Jap because Shaky Swanson had hurt his main man's girl real bad, and Jap is in Swanson's gang, the Schoolboys. So," Williams summed up the story, "Rebel jumped Jap."

"Is that clear to everybody, now?" Lieutenant Rock asked. And he laughed.

Behind Morales there was a stir of movement. Cool lunged in alarm as a white cat leaped onto Indian Red's shoulder. He was too late. Morales, the cat-fearer, flinched and looked at the cat on his shoulder. It walked down his chest and curled up on his lap.

All that hard work! Cool thought. *And now Morales will flip over a cat, and the show's over!*

But Morales, after frowning at the cat for a moment, began to pet it. Then, in shock at what he was doing, he raised his gaze to Kinsman's face.

The African commented: "He likes you. I've always said cats were a good judge of character."

"Even a cat can make a mistake," giggled Louie Diaz.

Morales ignored the mortal insult and continued stroking the animal. "I've always been afraid of cats," he admitted. "Like some people hate snakes. But with me it's been cats."

"But it's not cats now?" Kinsman asked.

Morales looked puzzled, and touched his forehead. "No! Dig that, huh? This cat don't bother me. How do you explain that?"

96

"The honey," said the African.

Morales stared at the cat. He did not answer, but sighed and scratched as if trying to comprehend something that was too much for him. He looked up finally, glanced around at the others, and settled his glance on Shamberger, the Picket Fence godfather from across The Wash.

"Level with me, Sham," he said. "Do you feel anything?"

Shamberger, long-faced and long-toothed, patted his belly. "Well, yeah. I got this feeling that I, you know, just had good news or something. Funny. . . . No big trip, but—"

"Anyone else have the feeling?" asked Kinsman.

Louie Diaz, the Dog Gang man, leaned forward to pick up two cigarette butts and toss them at the trash box. "Yeah, I dig what he means," he said. "I ain't spaced, but if somebody crossed my name off a wall and wrote his above it, I'd just say big deal, so what? I wouldn't even care." He sounded puzzled.

Breathing Man smiled and closed his eyes. "That's real cool, Louie. I've always said you had. The makings of a fine young man. You picked up your cigarette butts, too. That was nice."

Diaz grinned at him. "You're a cool old dude. And you got a real clean pad here, so why mess it up?"

Lieutenant Rock chuckled. "Funny, Louie, I never realized your mind worked that way. I thought the reason you messed things up was *because* they were clean."

"That's only when I'm on a bummer, Lieutenant. Anyway, how does anybody know why they do things? You just do them, right?"

Indian Red said, "You got to live the life to know the life."

One of the officers said: "The life would be easier if you guys stopped pounding on each other, wouldn't it?"

"But where are you going to stop?" asked Bread Williams. "I don't remember a time when somebody wasn't getting burned because somebody else was squaring for something. It's like Jap and Rebel. To stop it, you'd have to rewrite the history books!"

"Then let's burn the history books!" exclaimed Joshua Kinsman. "Let's wipe those old feuds from our minds and each sign a paper."

"What kind of paper?"

"A paper that says you believe in brotherhood, that you hold no grudge against anyone. That you recognize each other as leaders capable of controling your own clubs. And that you will channel the energies of your members toward good acts."

From his suitcase, Kinsman picked up a sheaf of papers, each bearing a red seal. "The papers are ready for your signatures. Does anyone object to signing?"

"I got a question," said Valenzuela. "What happens when we come down from this high we're on?"

"You aren't on a high, Mr. Valenzuela. A substance in the honey you've eaten has modified some circuitry in your brain. It's as though we'd pulled the fuse from a firecracker. The fuse may burn when someone provokes you, but the firecracker doesn't go off. Instead, you think about your options. If you've been assaulted, naturally you defend yourself. But if someone has insulted you, you laugh at him as a fool. If he has burned your car, that's a matter for the police. Now, if each of you signs, and keeps his word, nothing is going to happen."

"Turk Ransom won't sign," Diaz pointed out.

"Ransom is a more difficult case. While we wait for

him to come around, the police will keep him in line. In fact, he's not likely to be released from jail for some time. Sooner or later we'll get some of the honey into him, and he'll be a new man."

Lieutenant Rock set fire to another cigar. "Seems to me these boys are going to have a lot of spare time on their hands," he said. "And spare time leads to hard time."

"Spare time, Lieutenant?" asked the African. "What about school? Work-and-study programs? Jobs? Neighborhood beautification projects?"

Rock's gaze ran around the circle. "No objections?" he asked.

"I done pretty good in school," Morales said. "When I went, at least. If I finished high school, I could get a job with the County."

"My old man is a finish carpenter," said Diaz. "And his old man was a carpenter in Mexico. I hear they pay good."

"The union has an apprentice program," Rock told him. "You could go there half the day, go to school the rest. O'Conner, see about it, will you?"

The officer behind Diaz, looking dazed, said he would. "I'll take him over to the union hall when we leave."

Bread Williams said he'd worked in a body and fender shop, but before he looked for work he'd like to clean up some vacant lots in his turf.

Shamberger had an idea for raising organic vegetables on vacant lots. "Them organic food-freaks would buy stuff if you put up stands."

When all the reports were in, Lieutenant Rock said: "I've got a feeling that it's beginning to snow in here. But I'll do everything I can to help. Are you going to give these guys some honey to keep them from going bad on me again?"

"Each boy will get a small supply and a few candies. That should keep the lid on while I work. . . ."

"At what?" demanded John Tiffany.

Kinsman shrugged. "Negotiating," he said. "My main interest is in bringing certain national figures into this experiment. It will work. But where do we go from here? So I hope to talk this week to the President. As well as the Attorney General, the National Council of Churches, the National Corrections Board—"

"Just for openers," said Tiff, cynically.

"Of course I'm mainly waiting to hear from the President. I've already sent him a telegram, in case he hasn't learned of our work from the media. I know he must be a very troubled man. Certainly it's a very troubled world.

"But what if peace and joy came to it, by grace of a tiny insect no larger than the tip of your little finger?" He beamed into the television camera.

"Good question," Tiffany muttered. "What the hell *would* happen? Peace has never been tried before, my friends."

CHAPTER

18

A woman with a rough voice cried from the telephone: "What the hell do you people think you're doing?"

Cool held the telephone away and frowned at it. Then he said, still chewing toast,

"You sure you got the right number?"

"This—this *peace* honey, this *brotherhood* crap—! Who you trying to kid, baby?"

Cool reached for his coffee and swished some through his teeth. "I just work here, lady. Where'd you get my name?"

"From the television and newspapers, you peace-freak!" the woman said.

Entirely possible, Cool realized. Last night he, Aunt Josie, and the kids had watched the television report of the sewer peace conference, and of course Tiff had written it up and his paper had run a full page of pictures. His name and address had been mentioned again. Great.

"Hey, look, I'm a friend of J. S. Kinsman's," he said, "but I can't tell you anything. Why don't you call him?"

"In a sewer? No telephones in a sewer, sweetheart. That freak's just about wiped out my husband and my little business, and if we go under, I guarandarntee you we'll sue him!"

"Too bad. What kind of business?" asked Cool.

"We've got a gun shop. And here last night *three* customers called to cancel hand guns they had on back order! What the hell you got to say to *that*?"

"I don't know. That's your business."

The husky voice croaked a bitter laugh. "Yours too, sweetheart, if we sue you. Because all that Commie crap you and Kinsman have been giving out, it's got people relaxing about crime in the streets. *You* live in this town, *you* know it's not safe to walk the streets at night. And what about the junkies, and all those beasts breaking into houses, and people getting tortured and robbed and raped? You've *got* to have a gun to live here!"

Cool told her he didn't have a gun, but she said maybe he'd better get one, if he was going to keep on giving out propaganda like that. She hung up.

Cool went up to shave. He thought again about growing a beard and wearing shades. Crime in the streets began to sound like the gun shop people sniffing around for a target that looked like Hankins. But then he smiled, thinking about all the nice calls they would have, and how, eventually, peace would come and people would think of him as having been Kinsman's helper.

Before he finished, Janet came running upstairs. "It's a long-distance call, Uncle Cool!" She had her hair done up in two little spikes.

"For me?"

"Uh-huh!"

Cool ran down to the kitchen, shirtless and with his

jaws half black skin and half white foam. He said hello, and the operator said,

"I have a call for Mr. Walter Hankins."

"Uh, speaking."

"Sir, I have—"

Another voice rode in impatiently. "Hankins, this is Chief of Police Ernie Kerrigan! I'll write you a letter with all the details, but I live in a city two thousand miles from you and I need your help. I'd like to get some of that African honey. Here's my situation—"

"I can't get you any," Cool said. "I'll ask, but there isn't much of it, and—"

"The hell with that. It's a question of price, and my commissioners are ready to negotiate with your friend. I have twelve thousand cops under me, and they spend approximately seventy percent of their time handling gang problems. Murder one is out of sight, stat rape and forcible—we're setting records. If the price is right, I'd like about ten fifty-five gallon barrels of it, or the equivalent. I'll pay your friend's expenses to fly here, or I'll fly there and talk with him. I've already arranged for a gang peace conference."

"Chief, I sure want to help you. And I think pretty soon we can. But read the paper again. This is long range. The honey comes from Africa, a little bitty country there, and there isn't much. . . ."

It was queer to have a chief of police pleading for help from a seventeen-year-old black kid who was having trouble with math, and who had done a little time in honor camp a few years ago. But the chief sounded absolutely heartbroken that he could not get at least one barrel of honey immediately. He promised to make Cool an honorary captain of detectives, to make him Boy of the Year.

"Write me a letter," Cool said. "Maybe he's got

enough to send you some right now. At least for your-self. It makes you feel better, but it's not an upper, it's just food."

The chief sighed. "I'll write you," he said. "What's your zip code?"

With a shock, like no hot water in the shower, he re-membered that twenty-four million dollars' worth of queen bees were waiting for him at the bus station.

Two, four, six zeros.

At ten percent interest, somebody could make two million, four hundred thousand dollars a year without so much as getting out of bed in the morning.

What if he held out one bee for himself?

Could he sell it to a beekeeper somewhere?

As he understood bees from Mr. Kinsman, the Tulami queen would enter a hive from which the old queen had been evicted, and the eggs she laid would produce the small, solid-gold bees of Africa. And they would sip nectar from flowers and begin storing up their magic honey.

A second later he shivered, ashamed that such an idea could even occur to him. As though he had scratched a scab and found a bottomless well of pus in his body. Sheepishly, he flogged it from his mind.

Nevertheless, he'd better look in on the queens, let a little fresh air into the locker, before he touched bases with Kinsman today.

As he was pulling on a red tee shirt, Marvin entered his bedroom. On his dosage of Tulami candy, he looked like teacher's pet, neat and clean and happy.

"Uncle Cool, Aunt Josie says the phone's ringing off the wall. And there's some cars out in front and people are looking at the house. How come?"

104

Cool crawled over his bed to scowl down through the window. Sure enough, four cars were lined up in the street, and a white Continental that he recognized was slowing as a vacuously grinning white man inspected the house.

"There is no way I'm going out there and get hassled by all those freaks!" Cool snarled. Angrily, he stuffed wallet, handkerchief, coins, and keys in his pockets. "Listen, Marvin—tell Aunt Josie I've gone to look for work. You eat your candy this morning?"

"Yes, sir. Don't forget to bring me another piece for tomorrow. Sure do feel good, Uncle Cool. I want to be a good boy."

"You the baddest boy I know."

Cool raised the window at the end of the hall on the second floor. He leaned out, tugged on the scabby gray drain pipe nailed by plumber's tape to the shiplapped wall. Hoped it would hold his weight as, years before, it had supported the kid called Monkey in his nightly escapes from the house. Below him lay a yellow-green patch of devilgrass littered with toys; beyond, a picket fence, and the alley.

Cautiously he let himself down the wall. Six feet from the grass, he kicked away into a free-fall. Then he trotted across the lawn, jumped the fence, and caught a bus two blocks away. As it went blustering up the boulevard, like a smoking dragon, he saw other cars groping into his street, the drivers squinting out at the street sign.

Must be recess time at the funny-farm, he reflected, and they were all coming over here to play.

CHAPTER

19

Crossing the bridge, he reared up to stare down into the railroad yards. Far off, squeezed among lines of freight cars, he saw the little string of cabooses. He sat back, but grew restless. Was someone watching him? He had the feeling. He looked around and saw a middle-aged woman with a huge purse on her lap staring at him. Her glance dropped as their eyes met. Almost instantly, however, she sneaked another look, and he could read her face.

Q: Where have I seen that boy before?
A: On television.
Q: What shall I hit him for?
A: Some honey to use on my rotten son, or my alcoholic old man.

Three blocks early, he got up and left the bus by the back door.

In the bus station, the loudspeaker was bawling incomprehensible messages about cities and buses. Though he could scarcely understand Word One, people hurried to form lines, clutching parcels and chil-

dren. He gazed around, his lips puckered, then sauntered toward the bank of lockers where he had left the
queens. A man with a big, tousled, square head like a
bull's was fitting a dime into a small locker. He twisted
and removed the key. Wearing an orange nylon wind-
breaker, he passed Cool without a glance.

Cool crossed the room to a candy counter and bought
a newspaper. He went back and sat down near the
lockers to look things over. He wanted to be sure no
one was watching him. Pretending to read, he was suddenly startled into actually reading.

His picture was on page one, along with those of
Kinsman, Breathing Man, and some gang boys.

CRIME DROP! a caption cried hoarsely, above a picture of Captain, no longer Lieutenant, Rock.

SAVAGE LAB RATS BUILDING NEST! said another
caption, and the rats, scarred from old battles, looked
as happy as newlyweds in their wire love-nest at
U.S.C. medical center.

CLEAN UP, PAINT UP, WEEK IN GANGLAND. The
photo was of Indian Red Morales and a group of Nighthawks, painting out gang names and symbols on a small
white building.

Cool lowered the paper with a bemused smile. It was
working! Really working. Just as his morning candy bar
was at work in him, kindling optimism, quiet force, and
serenity. Underlaid, way down, by a sense of alarm, and
a doubt about where it would all end. For all this happiness was abnormal.

He went back to the newspaper. A famous evangelist,
a close friend of presidents, cautioned that it might be
the plot of a godless nation to trick America into disar-
mament.

The Honey Institute warned that strict tests should

be undertaken to guarantee the Tulami honey's purity. In the meantime, our native honey was man's most perfect food, and people should eat more of it.

Cool gazed around. A woman emerging from a telephone booth gave him an idea. He would call the Mission and see what Matt could tell him, meanwhile continue watching for spies. He shut himself inside the glass box, and dialed. Matt came on the line. Under his voice was a rattle of activity unusual in the Mission.

"What's happening?" Cool asked.

"Lucky you called before you came. This place is a nuthouse. Listen: Can't repeat this. A guy's already moving in to listen in, some nut in a beekeeper's bonnet. Holy tomato! Where are you?"

Cool told him.

"Good. Take a couple of hundred bucks out of the locker, the man says. Get two hotel rooms in the Five Points area. Use the names Gideon and Walter Beauregard—you're Gideon's son. Gideon will show up after dark. He's hiding in a different tunnel right now. You should see this place! They're looking for you, too. Get adjoining rooms if you can."

"Okay. I get the room and read the comics till he shows up. I think a woman recognized me on the bus."

"A lot of others will, too, unless you change your looks. Get some new clothes, he says, and wear glasses, not shades. After you get the rooms, phone the address and telephone number to me. Oh, yeah—be sure there's a phone in Gideon's room."

Cool came out, dug his key from his pocket and sought locker #375, corresponding to the number on the key. He inserted the key, turned it, and the gray door swung open. He drew a breath as he saw the queen cases neatly stacked exactly as he had left them, a million dollars per case. Also Kinsman's red book beside them.

He could think of little to do for the queens. All they needed was air, Kinsman had told him. Folding his newspaper, he fanned the cases. Then, with a glance behind him, he opened the red book. Take a couple of hundred, the man had said. He separated two of the bills, which clung together like new playing cards, and pulled them from under the brown paper band. He slipped them into his wallet. Then he closed the locker door and tried to turn the key.

He frowned. It remained fixed in the lock. Of course: It would take another quarter to turn and remove the key. He pulled out his change. There were so many nickels and dimes that at first he could not believe there were no quarters. But it was true. He could not lock the door until he crossed the room to the candy counter and got change.

His heart did a little skip. He felt sweat forming above his hairline.

A stout, busy-looking little black man in gold-rimmed glasses, carrying a large suitcase, moved in beside him. "Are you coming or going?" the man asked.

Cool had to clear his throat before he could speak "Coming. You wouldn't have a quarter for two dimes and a nickel?"

"No. Sorry. Whoo! Never see so many of the big lockers taken—" The man put his head against the locker to sight for the gleam of protruding keys. But there were none at all. "Everybody else looking, too," the man said, "Couple of buses just came in."

All Cool knew was that he'd better move fast. He thought of carrying the red book with him, but feared it would make him more conspicuous. The main floor was a jungle of travelers coming and going. "Azzabazz Oceanside and San Diego Gate 4," the loudspeaker droned. The announcement stirred up the ants, and small children were dragged by one arm toward a certain gate opening on a tunnel.

Putting his head down, Cool lurched toward the candy counter. He reached it and put his money on a green pad like plastic grass. But someone else just ahead of him gave the girl attendant a twenty-dollar bill for a dime candy bar, and she showed how she felt about it by sighing and making change very slowly. "Thanks a lot," she said bitterly.

"Would you—" Cool began.

"What?" she demanded.

"I need a quarter for a locker."

"We don't make change. There's a change machine near the coffee shop."

"But—"

"Sorry. Yes, sir? Can I help you?"

Cool muttered under his breath and looked for the coffee shop. He found the change machine, but what it did was to take quarters and turn them into dimes and nickels. Then he saw a different kind of machine beside it, which took dollar bills and returned quarters. He laid the bill under the plastic arbor and pushed it in. In a moment he had his quarters.

Weaving and side-stepping, he made his way back to the lockers. A bowlegged old woman in a pork-pie hat was trying to cram a suitcase into his locker, the only one with a key in it. Cool hastened up.

"Ma'am, I'm sorry—I already got— See, my stuff's in the locker already."

The old woman turned to peer at him through her thick glasses. She had a face like a bulldog's. "What?"

"I had to get change! My stuff's already in the locker, that's why yours won't go in."

"Take it out," the woman said. "First come, first served."

"That's right. And I was the first one here."

"You shouldn't leave it, then. It's not fair to other people. It's mine."

Cool finally nodded and told her humbly: "I guess you're right. Okay, I'll get my stuff out—"

The woman grudgingly gave ground, saying, "It isn't fair to other people. You should get your change first. It's not right."

"No, ma'am," Cool said, dropping a quarter into the slot and turning the key. He removed it, dropped it in his pocket, and ran off like a thief.

CHAPTER

20

Next stop: the Volunteers of America thrift shop.

Cool roamed a huge room like a disheveled gymnasium, filled with racks of clothing. In glass cases around the walls were dolls, wigs, curling irons, hot pads, costume jewelry—practically everything except false teeth, and he had the impression that if you carried a steak through the room, you would hear teeth clacking in a case somewhere.

He roamed the aisles, searching, till his eye was caught by a black suit of shiny material, with narrow black lapels. For ten years no one had worn suits like that except people who gave out religious tracts on the street. These people always were very neat and polite. Most of them wore spectacles and carried briefcases.

It would be the perfect disguise, because people tended to avoid looking at these apostles lest they be drawn into a discussion of the state of their souls. They were practically invisible.

Unfortunately, however, they all wore their hair quite short. An impostor with an Afro would be spotted instantly. So it was all or nothing. He slumped, realizing it must be all. The mission was more important than the man.

He made his purchases and changed clothing in a little dressing room at the back of the store. Five minutes later he left, a tall, slender youth wearing a narrow, dark suit, a pair of brown-and-white shoes, and carrying a scuffed brown briefcase and a secondhand Bible. He gazed up the street through a pair of secondhand spectacles that made everything look soapy and out of plumb. Into his briefcase were crammed his tennis shoes and other clothing.

Down the street he found a barber college. Grimly, he told the student barber to cut his hair two inches long. Afterward, he looked at himself in the mirror; he moaned softly. The point had been not to look like Hankins, and he certainly didn't; he looked like Malcolm X. Which was okay, except that if Malcolm X were living today he would probably be wearing an Afro, not a short cut like this.

He walked to the corner to wait for a bus. Fixed to the bench he saw a box holding some religious tracts and magazines. The final touch! He stole all of them, shuffling to the top a magazine called, *Salvation or Damnation?* Then he stood against the wall of the corner building, displaying the magazines, his briefcase at his feet like a faithful dog. No one looked at him. People peered down the walk as though they saw their buses coming. A surprising number of them, in fact, also carried religious tracts.

At the heart of the Five Points neighborhood was an intersection in the shape of a starfish. Cool had always liked the area because it resembled a foreign country. There was a Japanese bank, a Turkish bath, Chinese and Mexican restaurants, grocery stores where no English was spoken, and a police station where all they spoke was English. On the street you heard more Spanish spoken than English. It was not a good place for a black kid; but, of course, things were cool right now.

He checked out three hotels, all small and depressing. There were crisp, dead flies and dusty plants in the windows and the lobbies were full of sad old men picking at themselves and trying to kill time before it killed them. Then he came to one called the Hotel Satsuma, that looked clean and prosperous, small as it was. He went inside.

At the desk, an Asiatic was reading a Japanese newspaper. He looked at Cool with polite curiosity. Cool's spectacles made the man's face look fuzzy. "Yes, sir," said the manager.

"I need a couple of rooms for my, uh, father and I. He'll be along later."

The manager's head began to nod, like one of those plastic birds which dip up water from a tumbler. "Oh, uh-huh. Adjoining rooms?"

"That'd be fine. And one with a telephone."

"All of our rooms have telephones and television. First-class hotel. Most of our guests are Japanese businessmen. You got any luggage?"

"My father's got it. I just got our briefcases. We're with the Salvation Now people."

"I a Buddhist Now, myself," the manager said, with a smile. "The rooms are nine dollars apiece."

Cool felt uneasy offering a hundred-dollar bill, knowing most missionaries had never seen anything larger than a ten, and fearing that it might pull his front. But the manager merely popped it between his fingers, glanced at it, and made change. He gave him two keys with red fiberboard tags stamped 209 and 211.

Inside Room 209, Cool ripped off the spectacles and rubbed his eyes. They strained crazily to get back into focus. The room was small and neat, the walls cream, the trim pale blue. There was a double bed, a television set, and a dresser. On a small stand by the bed was a telephone.

He opened a door in one wall and went into the adjoining room, which was identical, except that it was trimmed in green instead of blue. Cool went back, locked the hall door, and sat on the bed looking out the window onto the roof of a building next door. Hankins' room; Hankins' world.

He wished you could make a career of disguising yourself and staying in hotels. He lay back with his arms crossed under his head and let the fantasy roll. Suppose he had a couple of thousand dollars in his pocket and all he had to do was travel around, eating in different places, listening to music, and making casual friendships. "I'm from Coast City, Betty—nice to meet you. I'm here for the track meet, maybe you heard about me—Micky MacNair, two miler."

Or, "I'm from Tulami, in West Africa, and I'm going to college next fall. If you aren't busy, why don't you and I rip a chop together tonight?"

He worked off his tight, brown-and-white shoes and wriggled his toes. Then sat up. Time to work! He reached for the phone and the manager's voice came on.

"I want to make a telephone call," Cool said. The man said to dial nine, then dial the number. Cool rang the foster home, and after bucking five busy signals, he got Aunt Josie.

"Hey, baby, how you doing?" Cool crowed.

"Walter! This phone! My stars! Where are you? What are you up to?"

"I'm at the Hotel Satsuma, on business, but don't tell anybody except Tiff. And I'm so clean you wouldn't know me from Malcolm X. That's all I can tell you right now. Just watch the news for further developments."

"Walter—"

"I can't talk any longer, Auntie, got a call to make for Mr. Kinsman."

He dialed the Mission ten times before he succeeded in touching bases with Matt. In the background he heard a hubbub. "Walter Beauregard, Matt. What's happening?"

Matt said guardedly: "Oh, hello, Smith. Listen, I'm busy right now. The television people are interviewing a man called Breathing Man."

"Crazy."

"Well, I'll tell you, Smith, why don't you mail me your best price on five gallons of disinfectant? And the lice powder in half-ounce packets. Oh, and one other thing—if you can give me the name of a reliable boy to do odd jobs, at the legal minimum, I'd appreciate it. Run errands, things like that. . . ."

Cool realized people were listening in, that he was probably asking for the name of someone who could take a message to Kinsman. Must be quite a problem by now.

"Sure," he said, "Little Pie Pastelito isn't working now. He could help you there. The phone number's 465-3426."

His wrist watch said: 2:20. Hunger pangs tore at him like a wildcat. He hurried downstairs and went looking for a restaurant. People on the street gazed curiously at him. He offered everyone a tract, but got no takers. He kept expecting someone to rush up and say, "Malcolm!

Man, we thought you were dead!" He found a Japanese restaurant and had two teriyaki burgers and a chocolate shake. Then he bought some magazines and newspapers and went back to the room.

At five o'clock, the sun still two hours from the skyline, he watched the news on television. Breathing Man, bundled up in overcoat, knitted cap, and scarf, was responding to questions from a small army of newsmen who stuck microphones in his face. Cool beat his fist into his hand, grinning, listening to the old man. Nothing he didn't already know, but wow—Breathing Man on television!

The sun sagged lower, he got hungry again, and went out for Chinese food. In the smoggy twilight he walked a while. He saw a bunch of Chicano dudes wearing Kung-Fu gang jackets, picking up trash in a vacant lot and throwing it in a yellow city trash truck. Los Tres men. Now he had seen everything! He went back to his room and read the evening paper.

Darkness settled into the streets of Five Points, and almost immediately there were four hard knocks on his door. Shoeless, he donned his glasses and coat, padded to the door and opened it. It was Captain Rock, looking very sharp in flared cuffed pants and a mod shirt with only a slight bulge under his left arm where he carried his gun. Grinning, he passed a hand over his molded blond hair.

"Hey day!" he said. "I was looking for a cat named—" he glanced at a card, "Beauregard—but I see I got the wrong room."

"I'll give Beauregard the message. What's happening?"

Rock came in and closed the door, looked in the other room, looked out the window, under the bed. He looked at Cool, and laughed. "Beautiful. Anybody else know where you are?"

"I told my aunt. She won't tell."

"I've got Kinsman and three big shots downstairs in my car. The big shots were waiting at the Mission. I've got six cars there to keep anybody from following me when I make the runs. Kinsman will come up, then one of the big shots. After they have their talk, the big shot will go down and be locked in the car again. Then another will come up. We're going to hit about sixteen of them tonight."

"What's he want me to do? Stay out of sight?"

"I think he wants you to sit in on the sessions and kind of—I don't know, size them up for him. He figures you know the territory better than he does."

CHAPTER

21

Moving briskly, J. S. Kinsman placed three chairs in a triangle. He wore his red jacket and fez, and his trousers had been freshly pressed. He laid a notebook and a fountain pen on one of the chairs. Cool watched him move to the window and stand gazing out thoughtfully.

"You want me to sit in—for sure?" asked Cool.

"Just watch and listen. Then take the gentlemen out through your room. You'd better change to your regular clothes, Cool. Otherwise you'll have to find a new disguise."

As Cool was changing, he heard a knock on Kinsman's door, a murmur of voices, then chairs creaking. Wearing his red tee shirt and flared gray pants, he sauntered in. A very large, white-haired man in a snappy gray suit was sitting in the third chair. His face was as red as sirloin, and he wore a white mustache two-hairs wide. He looked rich and successful. Tucked into his breast pocket was a wrinkled slip of paper marked: *Boarding Pass. First Class.*

"This is Mr. Tyler," Kinsman told Cool, and he introduced Cool as his associate. Tyler got up and shook Cool's hand warmly, smiling as though he had known him all his life. Cool was afraid he was going to say something about his being a credit to his race.

"I'm sorry to have to limit everyone to fifteen minutes—" Kinsman began.

"Fifteen minutes!" exclaimed Tyler.

"But if your basic plan seems right, we'll have other talks."

Tyler put his palms together as if in prayer, frowned a moment, then smiled.

"You're the doctor. Point One: The firm I head is the largest food-processing conglomerate in the world. Coffee, candy, bread, dairy products—if our plants shut down, America would starve in six months!

"Our offer is to set you up with the largest complex of beehives in the world. We will guarantee to buy all you produce. We will develop products using the honey in breakfast cereals, candies—you name it. Once we have a surplus, we'll open up the international market."

"I see. How would a person without the price of one of your products get the honey?"

Tyler hesitated, touched his nose, but went on smoothly, talking his way out of the corner: "Government-funded school lunches. Honey stamps in welfare programs. . . ."

"So we have the problem of selling the Government on the plan?"

"Problem? It's no problem. Our lobby—" Tyler's hand flapped like a bird.

"But the inevitable delays and watering-down, and the unnecessary profits. I think it will have to be a non-profit governmental arrangement."

Tyler's hands clenched on the chair arms. He leaned forward and spoke rapidly of free enterprise, the Profit Incentive, and so on.

Kinsman glanced at his wrist watch.

Tyler, beginning to perspire, produced a folded computer printout and read from it. ". . . Coming down to an annual minimum for you of six million dollars!"

Kinsman rose. "The basic problem, Mr. Tyler, is to provide everyone in the nation with a daily ration of honey. I'm not convinced that your plan focuses on that. Please leave your card with Mr. Hankins, however."

"I'll get back to you," Tyler said stonily.

Cool led the man into his room. He opened the hall door. Tyler handed him his business card, then gripped his hand. "We have a very forward-looking program for the minorities in my company," he said. "I'm sure there will be a place for you at the consultant level."

"Fantastic," Cool said.

The next man was a Warden Carruthers from an eastern penitentiary. He was a short but solid-looking man, built like a middleweight who could go as a light-heavy. On the tip of his nose was a whitish patch like frostbite.

"I'll lay it on you like it is, Kinsman. I'm not a correctional officer—I'm a zookeeper. I am in charge of the most dangerous animal in the world—the adult male. Compared to an adult male, a Bengal tiger is a house cat. Locking up the wilder ones is not the answer, but it is the one society has settled on."

"How can I help you?"

"By giving me enough of your Tulami honey to keep the men from going crazy and starting on killing sprees.

I figure it will help them make it to parole, keep them straight after they get out."

"But at this stage, warden, the problem is one of supply. First we solve that, then we dole it out."

"Of course." The warden thumped on the floor with his heels twice. "I made a little talk to the men before I flew here. I said I'd come back with the answer to a convict's prayer. I guess I've got to let them down, eh?"

"Tell them the golden queens are laying the golden eggs, and within a year, there should be honey for everyone who wants it. Needs such as yours are very high on my list. But at the moment—I'm sorry. But keep the faith!"

One of the unbelievers was next. He was a tall, swarthy man with a clipped beard and a driven look. His suit was obviously expensive, but wrinkled, as though he had just taken a nap in it. He frowned as he studied a paper he carried, and Cool had the feeling that he was a man who lived far back in his skull, fingering the maddening pieces of two jigsaw puzzles that had been shuffled together. He said his name was Hilgard and he was a psychiatrist.

"I am the director of a psychiatric association. I'd like to say, on behalf of our four hundred members, that we applaud your aims."

"Thank you."

"But that we want to raise a finger of caution. Your dream of bringing peace to the world may explode into a nightmare. Do you know what often happens when a compulsive eater is cured of his affliction through hypnosis?"

Kinsman chuckled. "Yes, but tell me again."

"He or she becomes an alcoholic. You see, the symp-

122

toms of his neurosis have been removed, but *the disease remains!* It breaks out in a new form. Drinking to excess, insomnia, drug addiction—"

"Possibly. But the person who continues to eat a small amount of honey is safe."

Hilgard grinned like a monkey. "Then the patient is now addicted to honey?"

"Spreading honey on toast is one of the milder addictions."

Hilgard bit his lip. "Another point. In all human beings there is a vast bank account of rage. These feelings are usually spent a nickel at a time, on small flare-ups, brief spats with one's mate, horn-honking in traffic. The sickest people of all are those who are unable to spend this kind of energy. Most of them become physically ill, often die. Others have to be institutionalized."

"In Tulami," said Kinsman, "we have no institutions."

Hilgard flashed other warnings—of lawsuits, epidemics of people going mad and hosing down crowds with machine guns. It was clear to Cool that he was a very worried man. He worried about these things happening, and he worried about having no patients. Cool could understand that. But wasn't it better to have a few unemployed psychiatrists than millions of miserable people?

Hilgard demanded a supply of honey sufficient to make a five-year study of its effects. Cool showed him out.

A three-star general set fire to a cigar and explained various ways the Defense Department could use the honey. The big one was to introduce the stuff into the enemy's food in some way. They would then lose all

123

will to fight. Then we would attack! Zowie! Crunch! Hot diggity! He was on his feet, shouting, waving his cigar, when Kinsman said coldly:

"Will you show the general out, Mr. Hankins?"

Captain Rock kept sending people up and bringing others from the Mission.

A big, lithe, crew-cut man with a tanned face and craggy eyebrows took the chair. He had an easy manner, talked easily, and gave the impression that nothing he said was very important. His name was Rhiles, and he was with the Firearms Clubs of America. He lit a cigarette, inhaled deeply, and for a half minute the smoke kept leaking out of his nostrils and mouth as though leaves were burning somewhere inside him.

"This country was founded on the ability—and the *will*!—the guts!—to fight," he announced. "America is a nation of fighters. Call us violent if you will. Call us—the hell with it. When those Commie bastards raise their heads, *anywhere in the world,* we're there to shoot them off!"

"Mr. Hankins?" Kinsman said, glancing at Cool.

Cool rose and motioned toward the door between the bedrooms. The rifleman rose also and handed Kinsman a paper.

"In addition to being president of the Firearms Clubs," he said, "I am a process server. This paper is a summons for you to appear in court to show cause why you should not cease and desist from—"

"Out," Kinsman said. "Out!"

He tore the paper in two. But as the pieces fell to the floor, he bowed his head.

"I am sorry. But if the Commies are your enemies, Mr. Rhiles, *you* are mine. I want to *change* people's heads, not shoot them off."

124

The air of the room grew gray and bitter with the tobacco the visitors smoked to burn off their nervousness.
Cool had to empty the ash tray several times. Kinsman
displayed little fatigue, but Cool was getting tired of it
all, the pitches, the twanging nervousness you somehow had to match to stay in tune. A big lawyer type
spoke of the danger of putting attorneys out of
business—an important profession like that. A guy from
a food and drug agency wanted *all* the honey for
testing—just like that!

And then at eleven-thirty, the Five Points district
quiet except for sirens hiving about the police station, a
few distant auto crashes, a bottle breaking in some
alley, Captain Rock himself came up.

"This is the last guy, now. He wanted to drive over
alone, and he's got letters that made me think I'd better
cooperate. This is a very big politician type. Though I
don't think I ever heard of him."

At a washbowl in a corner, Kinsman was refreshing
himself by washing his hands with an ice cube from the
water pitcher. His coat hung from the closet doorknob.

"Then how do you know he is very big, Captain?"

"His letters are from Washington. And we had a call
saying he was coming on a Government jet. His name is
Dr. Malachi."

Kinsman raised his head, and turned. "In the Bible,
Malachi was the Messenger of the Lord. Yes, this must
be the person I've been waiting for—the only one I can
really sell the queens to! The President's represen-
tative. By all means send him up!"

"Will do." Rock grinned. "Hang onto your fez,
brother. You've got a little surprise coming."

CHAPTER

22

The telephone jangled in Cool's room, and he ran in to pick it up. It was Aunt Josie. While they talked, he heard the new man enter and speak to J. S. Kinsman in a voice pitched so low that Cool could not follow anything he said.

"I got to get on the stick, Auntie," he muttered. "Yes, I brought my toothbrush. Okay, okay!"

When he went in, a powerful-looking man wearing horn-rimmed glasses and a neat black suit and red vest sat in the guest's chair. A heavy gold watch chain traversed his vest. His hair was close cropped, and a thin portfolio lay on his lap. Upon it lay a sheet of paper bearing a typed list. He was broad shouldered and had a thick neck and big hands, but looked like a college professor. Cool saw what Captain Rock had meant about a surprise, because the man was black. He had a smooth, broad face the color of dark oak.

Kinsman, busy with something in his briefcase, introduced Cool. "My adviser on certain matters." Dr. Malachi rose and shook hands with Cool.

"Young man," he said.

Young man, what? Cool wondered. But that was all the visitor said.

Kinsman came from the bed where his briefcase lay, carrying two tiny gold cups bearing the bee emblem. He handed one to Dr. Malachi, who looked into the cup.

"Brandy?" he asked.

"Brandy and honey. In Tulami, all important conferences start with honey."

"I see." The Messenger of the Lord carefully balanced the little cup on the wooden arm of his chair.

"Will you tell me a little about yourself?" the African black asked the black American.

"Certainly. First, my name is not Malachi." The voice was rich and leathery, as confident as a bugle blast. "I am a White House attorney. Anything I say has been cleared at the highest level. I have a law degree from Harvard University. My great-grandfather was a slave, my grandfather a sharecropper, my father a janitor. I went to college on an athletic scholarship, and I took a silver medal in the Olympics. Does that do it?"

"That's fine. I was curious that the Lord should send a black man, since I know of no blacks at the highest level. I gather it was a public relations gesture. What I want to know is whether you are empowered to make a deal?"

The Messenger solemnly raised his right hand.

Kinsman sipped his brandy and honey. "You're not drinking," he observed.

"No, sir. Until we've thoroughly tested this honey, we have to regard it as a dangerous drug. I'm assuming the reports we've been hearing and reading are true. About it's taming wild gang men and savage laboratory rats?"

Kinsman nodded. "They're true."

"Then we're dealing with an extremely potent drug. All that comes from the honeybee is not honey. There is also its poison sac. Just for example." The Messenger's eyes were growing keen.

Cool glanced uneasily at Kinsman, who was gazing fixedly at Dr. Malachi. Kinsman said: "You've heard the story about the princess who was too kindhearted to have a man beheaded? So she had his head cut off an inch at a time. Rather than cut mine off an inch at a time, why don't you make your statement straightaway?"

The Messenger raised the typewritten paper from the portfolio on his lap. He read.

"Point One: We demand all the honey and honey products you have brought into this country.

"Point Two: We want all the queen bees, at your asking price of a million dollars each.

"Point Three: No further Tulami honey products will be imported until we've completed our studies."

Through the window, Cool heard a drunken peal of laughter from a nearby bar, then a crash of glass. The room itself was silent.

"What do you propose to do with the honey?"

"Make tests with it—on animals, until it's proven safe for human consumption."

"And the queens?"

"Destroy them."

"Why?"

"Why fill our hives with honey that may be habit-forming or even toxic?"

"What would you do if I told you I had a pill that you could drop into a tank of water and turn it to gasoline?"

"Buy the formula and destroy it," said the Messenger. "For obvious reasons. For the same reasons, we must control this honey of yours. You have nothing to lose, Mr. Kinsman, and perhaps much to gain. We're giving you your asking price. But we must have everything."

"What you're saying," J. S. Kinsman stated bitterly, "is that you don't want universal peace. Various people today have told me why they don't want brotherhood to be carried too far—because it would be bad for business. But you've wrapped it up. You've admitted that sick minds and occasional wars are good for business."

Dr. Malachi frowned. "All I've said is that we want to examine the idea from every angle."

Kinsman stood up, finishing his drink, then walked to the window to gaze down on the side street. Cool chewed his lip, feeling pain in his own gut. Kinsman had come here expecting to be welcomed as a savior; but the Government had just chopped him down. He heard the Messenger clear his throat.

"I told you some things about myself. Why don't you tell me a little about yourself? So that I'll know whom I'm dealing with."

Kinsman said: "It's all been in the news."

"Not the matter of your being fined in London six years ago for child molestation. Nor of serving a year in a French jail on a drug charge."

Kinsman looked at him blankly. "What nonsense is this? I've never even been in England or France."

"Look at your passport," said the Messenger.

Kinsman, still staring at Dr. Malachi, walked to where his coat hung from a doorknob. He found a billfold in it and inspected it, puzzled. "This isn't mine."

"Oh, no? Look inside it."

Kinsman cracked open the billfold like a book and examined a passport he found there.

"It's false!" he exclaimed. "It's my picture on the passport, and the dates are right. Everything is right except the visas for England and France. When did you put it here?"

"Someone must have done it who came to see you. Odd. And if they've done that, I suppose they could also give you a police record in those countries."

Kinsman tore the passport in two and hurled it out the window. He dropped the billfold on the floor. Rising, Dr. Malachi went to the hall door, a big man in black.

"I'll be in town for a couple of days. I'm staying at a little motel called the Starlighter. Call me there if you change your mind."

Cool sat on the edge of Kinsman's bed. He wasn't surprised. He was a little surprised that Kinsman was surprised. Peace and kindness were such revolutionary ideas that people were afraid of them. Kinsman started taking off his shirt.

"Tomorrow is another day," he said.

"Sure it is," Cool agreed, rising. "Absolutely."

Trouble was, in Dogtown all days were the same.

CHAPTER

23

Late the next day there was a ring on Cool's telephone. The hours had ground at their nerves, and Kinsman displayed fatigue. He was still hoping for someone from Washington—the Vice President, the Secretary of State—who would denounce Dr. Malachi as a repulsive fake, a hustler. And there would be a solid deal, and a choir of headlines would sing, "Peace! Peace! Peace!"

But the person did not come, nor did the telephone ring.

Then the telephone in Cool's room shrilled, while a nut in an enormous beekeeper's bonnet was offering Kinsman a partnership in a string of honey-farms.

Cool hesitated, his hand on the instrument, not sure he wanted to let another swarm of hornets loose. But he finally answered.

"Uh-huh."

It was Dr. Malachi, and he explained that he was sorry about last night, and said it was urgent that Cool come to his motel at nine o'clock tonight. He felt that he could make things clear to him, where he had failed to explain them to the African.

Cool tried to brush him off, but he was insistent, yet charming and folksy. Cool decided, what the hell, there might be a ray of hope in it for Kinsman. He said he'd come.

Between customers, he told Kinsman about it. "It won't cost anything to listen to him, and Tiff will take me over."

"All right. Maybe he's ready to fall back to a line I can accept."

Later, Cool telephoned Tiffany. He told him to pick him up on a corner about ten blocks from the Satsuma. The fat photog showed up in his tilted sedan and shoved the door open.

"Get in, quick! It is you, isn't it?"

Cool took off his weirdo spectacles and shuddered. "I had to go underground to keep from being mobbed."

"So what's happening, man?"

"Nothing good. He could make a bundle, but that's not what he wants."

Tiff drove, waving one hand as he spoke. "He came on too fast. Everybody's scared to death. Who the hell wants peace, when the world's never had it? It's like somebody asks, 'You want scarlet fever, or a bad cold?' You're gonna say, 'Gimme a bad cold,' because you've never had scarlet fever."

The Starlighter Motel was in the suburbs, off a freeway. A woman behind the desk said that Dr. Malachi had checked out. "But if your name is Walter Hankins, there is a note for you." She took it from a pigeonhole.

Cool carried it out to the sedan and removed his glasses so that he could see to read it by the dome-light. It told him to proceed to the Gypsy Trail Motel. If anyone was chauffeuring him, this person was to leave immediately, not hang around.

"I guess that's you," Cool told Tiff.

"I was expecting it. I'll park a few blocks away and wait. The Gypsy Trail's a terrible dump. I covered a murder-suicide there once."

The Gypsy Trail consisted of a double row of peak-roofed cottages, with space for two cars between them. A palm tree grew at either side of the entrance. Beer cans were scattered along the walk and in the parking lot. It looked exactly like a motel where you would go to kill somebody and then shoot yourself. Yet, surprisingly, there was one very nice car, a sporty little pumpkin-colored Datsun, parked beside one of the cottages.

But it was not Dr. Malachi's cottage. His was Number Eight; the Datsun was parked before Number Seven, directly across the strip of oily gravel. Malachi opened the door as soon as Cool rapped, and shooed him inside. "Come in, come in."

He wore the red vest unbuttoned, and the black pants again; but his coat lay on the bed and he was shoeless. Yet he looked very ill-at-ease rather than relaxed. Instead, he looked as though he were working like a fool at relaxing. He was being everybody's average black man. He laid a heavy arm across Cool's shoulders and said,

"So, how you doing, cat? Will you have a beer? Got some chilling in the cooler."

And he cracked a couple of cans of beer, while Cool took the straight-back chair the Lord's Messenger motioned him to. Dr. Malachi lounged on the bed on one elbow while they drank their beers.

"There's a real cool set of wheels across the way," he said, after belching unashamedly. "Crack the blinds and look it over."

133

Cool strolled to the window and hunched to peer out at the car. The emblem, 240Z, sparkled on the stubby rear end of the car. It had a long hood that drooped for less wind resistance. Dr. Malachi was saying, as though reciting something he had memorized,

"—Mags and steel-belted radials, of course, and special cams. Develops one-fifty at fifty-six hundred, baby. AM-FM, tach, and all the rest. Notice the license."

The Datsun had vanity plates that spelled HONEY B.

"Also there are some credit cards in the glove compartment that might interest you. The gas card is good for two years; the bills will be sent to me. —Are you a religious man?" asked the Messenger.

He was looking at Cool's tracts. Cool sat down again and sipped some more beer. "Lately."

Chuckling, Malachi said: "Those are pretty square threads you're wearing, for a young fellow."

"I guess so." Should have changed to his other clothes, of course. He hadn't been using his head. Now he was going to have to work up a new disguise.

"Look in the closet."

Cool saw a door and opened it. He murmured when he saw the fantastic array of clothes in the closet—shoes, boots, coats, pants, even a couple of hats.

"They're all your size," said the Messenger. "I got the sizes from your aunt. A very fine woman. We'll see that she gets a little grant for her foster home."

Sitting up, he rested the beer can on the floor, rubbed his hands together, and said: "Okay! The nitty gritty. Sit down, won't you?"

His heart half-fire—the car, the clothes—but half-ice—the sellout he was going to be asked to take part in; Cool sat down.

"Some questions. Is Kinsman out for more money than I mentioned? Is that the trouble?"

134

"No, the deal is—"

The Messenger's mouth smiled. "Just quick answers. We haven't much time. Is he religious?"

"Not exactly."

"Does he put anything in the honey? Some drug?"

"I don't know. Don't think so. I'm on it. Just feel cool, not wired or anything."

"Have you seen the queens?" The puffy, almost Oriental eyes focused down on him like the lenses of a microscope.

". . . Yeah. At the press conference."

"Where does he keep them?"

Cool shrugged. "Don't know." He drank some more beer.

The Messenger's eyes were skeptical.

"How will Kinsman decide who gets them?"

"He told me he'll only sell to the Government."

Dr. Malachi uttered a bitter laugh. "I *am* the Government, boy! Didn't he understand that? What did he expect, the President himself to walk in?"

"He knows you're the Government, but he didn't like your deal."

"I realize I disappointed him. But, goddammit, he's juggling with nitroglycerine! We'll make our tests, run our studies, *then* start production. Not before! Doesn't that make sense to you?"

"It makes sense to me that the Chain Gang was banging on my head a week ago, and now everything's cool. And stuff he tells me, like no mental institutions in Tulami, no violent crime—that stuff."

"Tulami is one of the smallest nations in the world. Its problems are headaches; ours are a fractured skull. How can you compare them?"

Maybe he was right. Still, Cool was willing to give the honey a try.

135

"So you're going to shoot him down," he said. "What kind of brother are you?"

Malachi rose, drank some beer, and patted Cool's shoulder. "There's an allegory in a book by some Russian in which the pope sees Jesus walking down the street. The pope says, 'Get lost, baby! Get lost! Do you want to break our rice bowl?' "

"I don't dig."

"He means that practically all Christian churches are waiting for Jesus to come back. So if he came back, the churches would be out of business! Right? You better believe it. That's the situation we're in now. If that honey cools the world down too fast, a lot of people are going broke, and we'll have such a depression we'll all end up Communists."

Maybe so, Cool thought. But how could things be worse than they were right now? Just think: no more ghettoes, no more crime, no more Turks and Marvins and murder-suicides.

"Anyway," he said, "I don't see what I can do to help you, even if I wanted to."

"You could tell me where the queens are hidden. We'll get them anyway, but we don't want to have to go to court, blacken his reputation, or something, to do the job. The Man told me, 'Do the job.' That was about thirty-six hours ago. He called me this morning to ask what was taking so long."

"Well, I guess that's your problem," Cool said, standing up. He crushed his empty beer can and dropped it in a grimy wastebasket. "Would you sell out your father, the janitor?"

Dr. Malachi sighed. "I'd probably do just what you're doing. —Here, catch—"

Cool caught the key ring he tossed. The keys were gold, embossed with a Datsun emblem.

136

"Take the damned thing," grumbled the Messenger. "I'm not about to drive it back to Washington, and the man who put up the money knew it was speculative. I'll walk out with you."

"You're kidding!"

"No, I can't even return it."

In the warm night the car sparkled like a candy apple. Dr. Malachi watched Cool unlock the door. A breath of leather and new-car smells gusted out at him. He smiled and scratched.

"You *could* do one thing for me. It would look good in my report. Show the flag for a few days."

"Show the flag?"

"As Navy men used to say."

He pulled a small, silk, American flag from his hip pocket and tied it to the aerial. "There you go! Hop in. You're home free. And looking like a patriot!"

Raising both hands in a wave, he walked back to the cottage. The door closed. Cool got the little car started, swelled his lungs as he swung back, shifted, and headed for the street. He turned west.

He had only driven two blocks when he understood about the flag. It was to tell someone something.

Two cars pulled in behind him—car-plaque cars.

Then another car jammed in ahead of him, and he was squeezed between them, front and rear. The cars had been waiting for him to leave. The flag told them:

He wouldn't make a deal. Talk to him.

CHAPTER

24

The car ahead of him slowed until he was forced to stop. One of the trailing cars pulled up at his left, while the other charged up to his rear bumper and hung there. He saw Mr. Clean at the wheel of the car at the side. The man beside him motioned to Cool to park. Just as Cool pulled over, he saw Tiff pass, going in the other direction and apparently paying no attention.

Cool sat under the wheel, numbed.

Three men walked up to him, all of them wearing wide-brimmed white hats. One of them was the skinny dude called Sprinter. Sprinter pulled his door open.

"Hello, sir," he said. "We're firemen. This is a routine fire drill. Get out."

Cool crawled out, slanted a backward look after Tiff. The car was gone, two-way radio and all.

"Take the keys out, and lock the door," said Sprinter McGaw. "This is a mean neighborhood, man."

Cool followed orders.

"Now we get into the purple car with Turk. You set in the middle."

Cool did not recognize the driver, but the man in the

rear seat was Turk, all duded up again in mod clothes. He, too, wore a wide-brimmed white hat. Cool saw the gleam of his teeth as he made room for him. Sprinter climbed in afterward, and Turk told the driver to drive.

Like a funeral cortege, the three cars moved out, radios yammering black rock into the night. Turk told the driver to turn the radio off. In the swift silence, he laid a hand like an eagle's foot on Cool's knee.

"How you doing, man?" he smiled.

"Well, you know, man," Cool said, "I've felt better."

"Was there something you wanted to tell me?" Turk asked.

"Nothing you don't already know."

"Yes, there is. Where they at?"

"Where's what at?"

"Them bugs—them queen bees. That's all there is left to rap about, ain't it? Knew about the honey, I s'pose."

"No. I really don't know nothing, Turk. I didn't even know you were out of the slammer."

Turk took time to light a cigar. "Told you we was on the same side of the glass, Monkey. A well-connected brother named Malachi achieved my release today. As far as the honey, I hear some short-haired honkies with some Government agency found where it was hid and dumped it in the sewer today. Ain't that a gas?"

Something in Cool's breast wilted like a leaf of lettuce in a skillet. Without honey, there was no peace. Without peace, there was all the bad stuff there had been before. But his will clenched like a fist, as he thought: As soon as the queens are out and working, there *will* be honey! It's just a setback.

"So things jivin' back to normal fast, Monkey," Turk said, blowing out bitter cigar smoke. "But now we needs them bugs. The man is offering bread like I

never seen before, so I'll just say this now, so everybody understands: We wants them queens now, tonight, or I'm going to play you a tune with this little
bitty piece of piano wire—"

Cool saw a thin snarl of light chase across his lap as
the street lamps shone on a piano-wire noose with a set-
screw arrangement. It was just large enough to slip over
a man's head. Turk's face shone like rubbed black bone
as he said:

"So what you say, Monkey?"

"Head for the downtown Greyhound bus station."

"In a locker, huh?"

"Right."

"No need for all of us to go. You got the key?"

"Uh-huh."

Cool knew they would really torture him, and that he
would really break down under it, because the POW's
all said there wasn't a man born who wouldn't break
down. And it did not take long. What he hoped was that
Tiff would get suspicious and alert Captain Rock, and
an all-points would go out.

"Let's have the key, man," Turk said impatiently.
"You retarded, or something?"

Then Cool saw a beautiful light reflecting on the
metal parts of the car. It was ruby red, and it was coming from behind them. And, a block ahead, he saw another source of red light—in fact, three or four
sources—all of them dome-lights or spotlights on police
cars. The driver spoke calmly:

"You all get some kind of a paper from that Malachi
dude, Turk? Because we may need it, baby."

Turk tossed the piano-wire noose out the window.
"Pull over, Crazy," he said. "Don't be slow. Hankins,
meet us at the bus station in two hours. I think my man
can work it again. Get your ass out of here now."

CHAPTER

25

Tiff drove Cool back to the Hotel Satsuma. The photographer was upset at the news of the honey loss, and his pudgy hands kept clamping and unclamping on the steering wheel. They had hung around the scene long enough to see Turk and his friends on the way to jail. Cool had wanted to drive the Datsun, but Captain Rock, who had been alerted by Tiffany, had suggested that he let the police go over it first for bombs.

"I'm sorry I can't rap with you," Tiff told Cool, braking harshly before the hotel. "But I've got to get down to the jail and cover that business. And then I want to check with Breathing Man about the honey. Maybe Turk was just talking big, about somebody dumping the honey. . . ."

"Short-haired honkies," he said. "Sounds like Government men, all right."

"Hasn't Kinsman got a little supply in his room here?" Tiff asked, wistfully.

"Not that I know of. We were going back to the storm drain tomorrow."

Suddenly, the photographer pulled the keys from the

ignition. "Get me a couple of candy bars out of the trunk, sport."

Cool shook his head. "You don't *need* it, Tiff. You're still on honey. So don't get your bowels in an uproar. Besides, there's still the honey in the hive. I'll have to get that in the morning."

Tiff started. "Hey, that's right! Let's go. No time like tonight!"

"The railroad guards would shoot us if they saw us prowling around. First thing in the morning. Thanks, Tiff, you really saved my life."

Tiff pointed a finger at him. "And don't you forget it, if you come across some more of those honey bars!"

Upstairs, Mr. Kinsman was standing before the window. His head was bowed. He could see Cool's reflection in the glass, and did not look around.

"I never dreamed," he said in a slow, deep voice, "that I would have such trouble giving peace to the world."

"Don't forget about Jesus," Cool said.

"Poor old Breathing Man called. He said they've destroyed my honey supply. Poured the honey into the sewer and trampled the honey bars into the sand. He was crying."

"Turk Ransom told me."

"He's out of jail?" Kinsman turned, surprised.

"That honky black, Dr. Malachi, got him sprung. But he's back again for kidnapping me."

"I think he'll probably stay this time. Dr. Malachi would be afraid to use him again."

"They still want the queens, though."

"True, but he failed him. Indian Red called, too. He said he's out of honey and doesn't know what his key men will do if they don't get their ration tomorrow."

142

"They get all uptight when anything changes," Cool told him. "They're bad dudes, but inside they're scared all the time. There's honey in the hive, isn't there? Tiff said he'd take me over to the railroad yards in the morning."

"There's only a few days' worth in it. The combs were nearly empty when I left, and the bees won't have had time to store up much more. But it might tide us over until public pressure forces the Government to deal with me."

"Hey! How about telephoning Tulami to ship us a barrel?"

"Importing cocaine would be easier. They'd seize it at the port of entry. In the morning I'll go back to the storm drain. If you'll bring the hive there, we'll portion it out and hope for the best."

Cool woke once with a nightmare. He sat up, whimpering. The room was dimly lighted by the street glow. He had been dreaming that a thin silver snake had wrapped itself around his neck and begun to strangle him. It was a long time before he got back to sleep, and at daybreak the telephone woke him again.

"Hi, skipper!" Tiff's high voice wheezed. "Hit the deck. I'll be over in fifteen minutes and take you to the Pantry for breakfast. Then we'll go over to the railroad yards."

"Man, it's only six-thirty!" Cool croaked; but the newspaperman had already hung up.

They ate at the counter of an all-night restaurant popular with cops and newspapermen. On the black grille steamed huge mounds of hash-browns, bacon, and sausage. Tiff ordered eggs, sausage, potatoes, and toast, devouring the food as though he had had a tip the place was going to be raided. Sucking a tooth, he gazed vacantly at Cool, a frown creasing his pallid forehead.

"I got that antsy feeling again, sport. —Come on, let's get that hive. Hup, hup."

Cool, only half-finished, carried a couple of slices of toast with him.

As they drove over to The Wash, Cool looked down into the railroad yards. His eyes swept the latticework of rails and clusters of freight cars. Startled, he said: "Slow down!" A knot of anxiety hardened under his wishbone.

Tiff pounded angrily on the wheel. "It's gone! Right? Dammit, I *wanted* to get it last night! I *told* you—!"

Tiff parked. There was a narrow sidewalk. Cool jumped out and leaned on the concrete railing. There were hundreds of cars down there, so many it was hard to distinguish one kind from another. But finally he realized that nowhere was there a line of cabooses.

The cabooses had left.

CHAPTER

26

Tiffany parked in the smoky jungle of small factories on the far side of the bridge. He switched on the radio-telephone under his dashboard and started making calls. After two false starts, he reached the dispatcher's office of the Southern Pacific Railroad.

He explained that he was a newspaperman and was doing a story on old-time cabooses. "You don't see them like you used to. Didn't you have quite a few of them parked here last week?"

He listened.

"Vacation homes, eh? Town of Eureka, in Northern California?"

He listened some more. Early-to-work traffic was clotting up. "About twenty-five-hundred dollars per car, but they're sold by the ton. Uh-huh. Would you know when they left?"

All at once his gross body heaved upright. "Is that a fact! Only an hour ago. Then they'd still be in the area, right? What I might do, I'm a photog, I might try to grab a picture of them as they pass. Could you tell me about where they'd be right now?"

Listening, he licked his lips as though he were already tasting honey.

"Right on, sir," he said. "Carson Grove. Thank you very much."

He started driving, staying off the freeways, which were jammed like parking lots at this time of the morning. He explained that the old cabooses were collected for a while, then moved to vacation areas like Northern California, where people bought them, took the wheels off, and turned them into homes in the woods. They were picking up a few more cars at Carson Grove, so if the damned traffic did not stop them—!

He kept the little sedan darting like a rat in a basement, along side streets, running signals, finally cutting onto a freeway after they had escaped the heart of the city. Here the out-traffic moved well; inbound was still jammed up.

They climbed a barrier of brown hills and dropped into a vast basin brimming with morning smog. Beyond a sea of housing tracts, schoolgrounds, and shopping centers, was the old railroad town of Carson Grove. Now it was just another community of cheap houses and skinny Chinese elms.

The sedan gunned along. Tiffany swerved down a ramp. A sign flashed by: CARSON GROVE *Population 13,567.* Tiff squirreled along side streets, boomed into one that dead-ended at a small stucco railroad station. He wheeled into an almost-empty parking lot.

"There they are!" Cool yelled, pointing. On a siding only a few hundred feet south, a yard engine was pushing a string of fifteen or twenty cabooses toward the station.

"Do you see yours?"

"The blue-green one! Jeez, if they've locked it—"

146

Tiff grimaced. "Gimme two minutes to tie the station master up in conversation. Then go! Break a window if you have to."

It was hard to look innocent when his veins were bulging with excitement and his ears were rigid with anxiety. The blue-green car was no longer the last in line; it was third from the front, now. Standing by a dusty shrub, Cool waited a couple of minutes, then walked down the parking lot. The first cars passed, clanking and squeaking. He crunched across the coarse gravel to the tracks. The car's weight made the ground shake. He saw a man atop a car, facing the rear. He clutched the grab irons and swung onto the platform.

He tried the door—hallelujah! Slipping inside, he sniffed the ancient stirred-up dust. He climbed the ladder to the cupola. A thought hammered him behind the ear: What time did bees go to work? Would the workers all be gone? Would they be charging around looking for somebody to sting?

Cautiously, he poked his head above the floor level. A few bees swam aimlessly in the air, and through the glass he could see bees inside the hive.

He stepped out on the floor, ducking his head as bees hummed about. He found the walnut case and clenched his jaws as he approached the hive. He brought it down squarely, fumbled for the small padlock, and slipped it through the hasp. *Click*, and it was ready to travel.

A bee stung him on the back of the neck. Another was crawling over his hand as he climbed down, and he waited for it to sink its stinger, unable to brush it off. It stung. He was on the platform, backing down the steps, stepping off onto the gravel.

"Hey, kid!" A railroad man with an iron rod in his hands yelled at him from up the tracks.

"It's all right. He's with me," Tiff called from the station's boarding platform.

"Oh, it's all right, huh?" the railroad man retorted.

Tiff, raising a camera, took a couple of shots of Cool, then of the railroad man himself. Then he jerked his head toward the car. Cool took the hint and walked toward the parking lot.

Tiff opened the trunk and said: "Can you open it for a minute and get me some of that honey? I'd lick it off a dog's back to get that fat feeling off me."

"You'd get stung. This hive is full of *bees,* man."

As he drove, Tiffany telephoned ahead to J. S. Kinsman.

"We've got it, we're on the way. Shall we meet you at Breathing Man's pad? And why not call Captain Rock and have him bring the gang men there? You can give them their rations. And look, maybe you ought to call one of the people who want to buy the queens and let him sit in on it, then make your deal."

"Says he will," Tiff grunted, driving grimly.

CHAPTER

27

"You understand," said Kinsman, "that this is the last honey I can give you for a time. But keep the faith. Soon we'll have the bees out and producing."

They sat in a circle in the vast, echoing storm drain—seven gang men, Kinsman, Breathing Man, Cool, Tiff, Captain Rock, and a weird-looking man wearing a bee-keeper's bonnet. A gauze of fine net obscured the features beneath the broad brim of the hat. His name was Culpepper, and of all the high-powered people the African had listened to, he had made the best offer: A million dollars per queen and a share of the profits of his firm, which was the biggest honey-producing company in the country.

On Breathing Man's card table rested several pie pans, in which were a number of dripping combs. Each was only partly filled. Culpepper had brought a smoker and had tranquilized the bees before robbing them of their honey. Then the hive had been locked up again.

The boys had washed their hands and been given plastic spoons with which to dip into the comb that

Kinsman had placed in the golden bowl. They were nervous, and Indian Red had a swollen left eye. One of his men had jumped him that morning.

Kinsman told them to dip in. Tiff was the first to partake of the honey. Only he and the gang boys ate it. The police officer spoke after they had finished eating.

"The honey's going to run out. I guess you guys know that. But there's no reason you can't stay in the programs we've got you in now, right?"

"Right on," said Bread Williams, waiting with a goofy smile for the good feeling.

"The stuff don't look the same as the other," said Morales.

"That's because it was produced from different flowers," the African pointed out. "At home, they sip the nectar of a number of tropical flowers."

They talked about that for a while. Obie Valenzuela chewed his lip. Another boy poured a thin silver chain from one palm onto the other, like a trickle of water. Culpepper said:

"May I?" Raising his veil briefly, he took his first spoonful of honey, smacking his lips. He looked faceless, like a figure in a monster film. "We haven't discussed how well they produce."

"Less well than Italians or blacks, but very well. For their size, better. It's possible that a cross between a larger bee and the Tulami—"

Cool found himself twisting the bee ring on his finger. "I better give you this while I think of it," he said.

"Keep it, my boy. Put the hive in your back yard and make it a project. You've lost some of the bees, but the queen will replace the workers you've lost."

Cool pushed the ring back on his finger. Hearing a

crackling noise, he looked up quickly. It was somehow an ominous sound—the crackle of Tiff unwrapping a candy bar. He was eating the bar in great bites, like some monstrous ant consuming an enemy. Fear and doubt twisted in Cool's bowels like a snake. Tiff froze, staring at the chocolate crumbs on his fingers in shock.

Everyone was beginning to look at the photographer.

"What's the matter?" asked Culpepper, leaning forward with a graveyard chuckle. "Isn't that old black magic working this time? Has something gone gespritz?"

Tiff's lips stopped moving; he pouted like a small boy. "I'm hungry, that's all," he muttered. "Just like old times. I could eat a warm horse."

"It's simple," said Culpepper, rising with a papery rustling of bee garments.

"I don't feel one damn bit different, man," said Morales. And he kicked out at a black-and-white cat near his feet.

"It ain't the same stuff," Valenzuela complained.

"But it was produced by the same bees!" protested Kinsman.

"The same bees, but different flowers," laughed Culpepper, drawing a document from a coat pocket and ripping it up. "I'm sorry, Kinsman—no deal. I should think you'd have done your homework before you put it on the market."

"But I did! We've used it for generations—"

"Not *this* honey—your native honey." Culpepper looked as though he enjoyed being the bearer of bad news. Cool strained to read the face behind the veil, but his head could have been a styrofoam skull on which to store wigs.

"Go back and do your homework," said Culpepper.

"Eliminate certain flowers from their diet. Find out which flower they need to work their magic. Then find out where it will grow in this country. Then get in touch with me. You have my card."

The group around the table watched him start down the tunnel. He turned back. "If you want," he said, "I'll take those queens and get them to working in our hives. Otherwise they'll die, of course. We can make a deal later, if you come back. *If*," he repeated.

Kinsman raised and dropped one hand. "Cool? Will you give him the queens?"

"I have my car here," said Culpepper, beckoning to Cool.

The gang boys were getting up. "Keep the faith!" Kinsman urged them. "It won't be long. I'll try to ship some honey to you."

Cool lingered, reluctant to follow Culpepper. The African rose and gripped his hand. "I'll be gone when you come back. There's no time to lose, and perhaps Mr. Tiffany will give me a ride to the airport."

"Any you guys want a ride?" Captain Rock asked.

The boys shrugged and went with him to the ladder.

Cool patted Breathing Man's shoulder. "I'll see you tonight," he said. "I'll bring you some ribs, okay?"

"Ain't that a shame?" said Breathing Man, as though he had not heard.

Kinsman was beginning to pack. "Cool, I'll swing by the bus station and pick up that, er, book you're keeping for me," he decided.

All the way to the bus station, Cool kept trying to see what Culpepper's face looked like. He had the feeling that it might be the bug-eyed visage of a giant red hornet, or some natural enemy of the honeybees of peace and good will. But he could never quite make it out.

All he knew for sure was that things were back to normal.

Yet not quite. For they had all tasted briefly the delicious honey called peace, had had a dream of brotherhood. And perhaps, when a Chain Gang man offended a Farmer, or a Nighthawk insulted an Elegant, they would both remember Joshua Smith Kinsman, that he had been here and had promised to come back, like Jesus. And then they might have the feeling again, and decide to wait, and hope, a while longer.